My Lady, Will You Dance?

Viennese Waltz

Sofi Laporte

Copyright © 2023 by Alice Lapuerta.

All rights reserved.
No part of this book may be reproduced in any form or by any electronic or mechanical means, including information storage and retrieval systems, without written permission from the author, except for the use of brief quotations in a book review.

This book is a work of fiction. Names, characters, businesses, organisations, places, events and incidents either are the product of the author's imagination or are used fictitiously. Any resemblance to actual persons, living or dead, events, or locales is entirely coincidental.

http://www.sofilaporte.com

Editor: Julia Allen
Proofreaders: Jessica Ryn
Cover Art: Covers and Cupcakes

Chapter One

Whenever the smell of mince pies and roasted chestnuts filled the air, Mirabel knew that Christmas was just around the corner. Snowflakes pirouetted from the sky, adorning the sooty roofs of London's townhouses with a gossamer white lace, conjuring a sense of glamour, a touch of enchantment that was unique to the season. Eager young boys careened down the icy streets, while little ones hauled sledges up the frozen slopes in the parks. If this bitterly cold weather persisted, it seemed entirely possible that the Thames would freeze over, and a magnificent Frost Fair would be held upon its surface.

The upcoming Christmas season was eagerly anticipated by one and all.

But not by Mira.

Mirabel Taylor was dragging buckets of steaming water, taking out the slops, polishing the silverware, waxing the floors, washing the windows, stoking the fire, clearing the grates, and soaking the laundry in lye.

For Mira was a housemaid at 24 Park Street, Mayfair, at the grand residence of Lord and Lady Cullpepper, and their daughter, Miss Rose Cullpepper.

Since the time before Christmas was one of the busiest of the year in the Cullpepper household, with dinner parties, soirees and routs to prepare, maids like Mira were given no respite. The bell was constantly ringing, and Mira was running, fetching, scrubbing, brushing, dusting, and washing from dawn to dusk.

It was indeed a busy time, this time before Christmas.

Lord Cullpepper's card party was a great success. He was lauded as a first-class host, who served his guests excellent wine and a superlative dinner, and whose card tables were always decked with brand-new cards. It was well past midnight and into the early hours of the morning when the last guest finally left.

Mira had wiped the tables, swept the floors, cleared the grates, and sprinkled salt on the wine stains on the damask tablecloths.

"If people had to clean up their own spills and were aware of the work it takes to get red wine stains out of snowy white fabric, they'd be more careful when drinking wine," she muttered to herself as she removed the tablecloths and put them in a basket in the laundry room for the maid to tend to in the morning.

Mrs Holt, the housekeeper, took one look at Mira's tired face and pursed her thin lips. "Have you had a morsel to eat yet, Mira?"

My Lady, Will You Dance?

Mira wiped a strand of hair away from her forehead. "Not yet, Mrs Holt."

"Then sit down and have some tea. You must take better care of yourself. I can't have another maid falling ill now that both Maggie and Renata are down with the flu. That would be a disaster, especially now." She handed Mira a steaming cup of tea.

"Yes, Mrs Holt. Thank you, Mrs Holt." Mira gratefully accepted the cup and sat at the long, oaken table where the servants dined. Though strict, Mrs Holt was a kind woman who took good care of the servants under her.

"And speaking of Renata," Mrs Holt continued, "we will have to redistribute your duties while she is bedridden. Lady Cullpepper has ordered you to take over her work."

Mira set down her teacup with a clatter. "But Mrs Holt, where will I find the time? Renata is Miss Cullpepper's abigail. I simply do not have the time to be a lady's maid on top of everything else."

She would have to look after Miss Cullpepper's person, dress and undress her, care for her wardrobe; darn, sew and wash out stains from the muslins, fine linen, lace, and silks. All this would have to be done in addition to all her other duties.

"You are to take Renata's place temporarily until she is well again. For the time being, I will hire another to take over your duties, for it is easier to find housemaids than trustworthy abigails. You have stood in for Renata before when she had to take leave to visit her ailing mother. Lady Cullpepper was very pleased with your work then." To Mrs Holt, the matter was decided.

Mira frowned. A lady's maid was expected to dance attendance to her mistress day and night, every day of the week. "But Mrs Holt, you know I cannot do that on weekends. I have a special arrangement with Lady Cullpepper in this regard."

Nothing in the world would induce her to give up her free day, that one day a week that she could spend with Miss Pearson and her little Clare. It had been the condition upon which she'd begun work in the Cullpepper household.

Mrs Holt rubbed her forehead. "I know that, Mira. But we must make the best of the situation here. Christmas is almost upon us, and this season promises to be busier than usual. Starting tomorrow, you will tend to Miss Cullpepper. We will see how things develop from there. There, now. It is late. Finish your tea and go to bed." Mrs Holt got up and retired to her room.

Mira was about to do the same when Emma, Lady Cullpepper's abigail, and Nancy, the head housemaid, entered. They both dropped into chairs and helped themselves to tea and biscuits.

"What madness this is! The entire household has turned upside down. Not just with Lord Cullpepper's card party and the upcoming Christmas celebrations, but with her Ladyship." Emma groaned. Even though she was an upper servant and usually ate with the butler and housekeeper because of her higher rank, she enjoyed gossiping with all the other servants in the household when the housekeeper was out of earshot.

"Tell us, what has happened?" Mira put the teacup in the sink for the scullery maid to wash.

"Has Mrs Holt gone to bed?" Emma turned her head to check that the housekeeper had indeed retired. "Very well, then come closer and hear the latest gossip."

Everyone crowded around the table.

"Her Ladyship intends to drag Miss Cullpepper to every single ball in town," Emma told them. "My lady said, 'Miss Cullpepper will be married before the year is out, so help me God.' I know this for a fact, because I was standing next to her when she said it."

"Poor Miss Cullpepper," muttered Nancy, who'd worked with the Cullpeppers since Miss Cullpepper's birth. "We all know how she hates balls. Why can't they leave her alone, what with her anxiety and fainting spells. She has such a fragile nature, poor child."

"But how is she ever to get married if she doesn't go to balls?" Mrs Bates, the cook, chimed in.

"And with Lady Cullpepper being so persistent. Have you heard the latest news?" Emma leaned in to say in a stage whisper.

Everyone, including Mira, leaned in as well.

"She has set her sights on none other than Lord Atherton as her son-in-law. He only recently came into his title and fortune, did he not?"

There was a collective gasp.

"I can't imagine anyone wanting to marry that one, despite his wealth and status. Of all the things one hears. But that will prove to be an impossibility," Nancy contributed.

"Why?"

Emma snorted. "He's a marquess. That's just below dukes. Impossibly high in the instep. He'll end up choosing a duke's daughter or a princess to marry. Our poor Miss Cullpepper, the daughter of a mere baron, has no chance, no matter how hard Lady Cullpepper tries. He is a league too big even for our mistress."

"It would be for the best," Mira said as she set down her cup. Even she had heard of Atherton, and it had not been good. "Really, it would. Miss Cullpepper deserves someone who appreciates her. Not some cold-blooded lord."

"Mira has a point," Mrs Bates said. "They say he is a philanderer of the worst kind."

"Poor, poor Miss Cullpepper!"

"He may be the worst philanderer in all of England, but they also say he is oh, so wonderfully handsome." Emma folded her hands in front of her and sighed.

Mira shook her head. "What's the point of him being so beautiful if he's chipped out of marble? They call him the cold marquess. He has no heart at all. Even if he were the most eligible bachelor, who would want to be married to a slab of marble?"

"Poor Miss Cullpepper," Mrs Bates repeated.

"Mira is right. Who'd want a heartless, cold marquess to warm their bed? At least I have my Ben to turn to, and he is as warm as an oven." Nancy giggled.

"Oh, hush you!" It was no secret that Nancy and Ben the footman were a couple. Emma had a sweetheart from her hometown whom she planned to marry next year. Mrs Bates, the cook, was already happily married. And even Mrs Holt and Mr Brown, the butler, had been stealing glances at each other lately, with strange blushes on their cheeks. Her Ladyship had no inkling what was going on under her own roof.

"What about you, Mira, do you have a sweetheart?" Emma asked.

"Surely you must have had a sweetheart. A girl as pretty as you," Nancy said teasingly.

Mira took a sip of her tea and found it too cold. She put the cup down and stood up, straightening her apron. "I shall turn in for the night now."

She fled from the kitchen, away from the pitying looks that followed her.

"...and she is such a pretty little thing..." Mrs Bates whispered. "What a shame."

Mira slammed the door behind her.

OF COURSE she'd had a sweetheart.

Once.

A long, long time ago.

In another time, in another world.

A love that was as ephemeral as the mist that hung over the cliffs in Cornwall.

But that was neither here nor there, and it was better not to think about it.

Mira unconsciously rubbed her ring finger, which was empty.

Sometimes she still dreamed of Cornwall.

Of him.

Feverish, colourfully vivid dreams where the sea was too blue, the meadows too green, and the marigold flowers too bright an orange. She saw his unruly head, the crooked white teeth in a mouth pulled back into a cheeky boyish smile, and an imp dancing in those mud-green eyes. An outstretched hand grabbed hers and pulled her along, and they ran, ran across the meadow, stumbling and gasping and laughing, until they reached the old yew at the top of the hill. Below them, the sea sparkled and shimmered in every shade of green and blue.

"You and me, Mira. You and me." His voice was husky.

She smiled at him and he cradled her head in his hands and kissed her on the lips with a tenderness that left her gasping.

She felt the roughness of his fingertips, the warmth and softness of his breath; breathed in the smoky smell of the forge, of leather and heated metal and ash.

That smell, good heavens, how could she have forgotten it?

She took his right hand and planted a kiss on his scarred back.

And she felt the happiness spread again to the tips of her toes.

She'd forgotten what it felt like to be truly happy.

It was so real, surely it had to be?

Then it hit her, the gaping emptiness. The longing and the homesickness.

Kit.

Home.

Kit was her home.

Always had been. Always would be.

Clouds gathered over the gnarled branches of the yew tree and a clap of thunder ripped through the sky. No, it was not thunder, but cannons, and fire, fire everywhere, burning everything, including Kit.

"Kit!"

She screamed his name, but there was a void, a staring black void where he had stood a moment ago, with such unbridled joy and tenderness in his eyes.

He was gone.

Again, the thunder.

She put her hands to her ears and whimpered.

Her whole body shook so violently that the metal frame of the bed shook with her.

A dream. It was only a dream.

But outside, it was as if the gates of hell had opened.

He took her in his arms and held her tightly, rocking her back and forth, to make her forget her bad dreams and her fear of thunderstorms.

"Hush now, Mira, hush. It will pass soon."

No one had done that for a long time.

She'd had to do it herself. Her arms wrapped around her torso, but it wasn't quite the same.

Her hands shook as she hastily wiped her wet cheeks and jumped out of bed to close the small attic window that had been thrown open, letting a gust of rain and wind into the small room. It took her three tries.

With trembling hands, she lit a lamp, went to the chest of drawers, pulled out the bottom drawer and rummaged through it. In a small bag, carefully wrapped in a cotton handkerchief, was a small wooden box containing her valuables. Where was it? She hadn't looked at it for months. She hadn't lost it, had she? A sob escaped her. She rummaged through it, her fingers stumbling over cold iron. She clasped the small iron ring and pressed it to her cheek.

The only bit of Kit she had left.

"Look: the loops are intertwined to represent the joining of two souls. It is a Celtic love knot. It means Serch Bythol."
"Eternal love," Mira whispered.
"Will you marry me, Mira? I'm of age now and I'm sure Miss Pearson will give her permission for you to marry me. She will. She must! I can start building a little cottage for us, right next to hers, so we won't be a burden to her. Much as I love her cottage, it is too small for us. One day we will have a child, won't we?"

Mira stared blindly at the ring in the palm of her hand.

They'd had a child.

And Kit had never known.

You and me, *Mira. You and me...*

The door opened, and Nancy, with whom she shared the room, entered.

"Mira, are you well? You look awfully pale."

Mira climbed back into her bed and pulled the blanket up to her chin.

"I'm fine, Nancy. Don't mind me, please." She lay down and stared at the ceiling.

My Lady, Will You Dance?

It had been seven long, lonely years.

In all that time she'd never had a dream that was so real.

Old dreams of love from a time that would never return.

Maybe it was time to let them go.

Chapter Two

"Mira! Where is that girl?"

Mira threw the rag back into the bucket and sighed. She rubbed her head. That storm. That dream...

Kit.

Only this morning she'd thought she'd seen a boyishly tousled head emerge from the crowd around the stalls in Fleet Market, a cheerful whistle on his lips, a branch of evergreens on his shoulders. She'd dropped the sack of apples she was carrying, slipped on the ice as she'd scampered to collect the apples that bounced down the street, and nearly sprained her foot.

It hadn't been him, of course.

It never was.

It was the tousled head of an errand boy in livery. He'd been the same height, though. The same slender build, the same broad shoulders. The same cheeky whistle on his lips.

But Kit would be seven years older. No longer a boy.

And she was no longer eighteen.

She had to stop searching for him.

"What folly is this," Mira growled, rubbing her elbow. "Chasing after wisps of dreams."

It was the atmosphere, of course. The celebration that hung in the air. The snow that lay like a silver blanket on the rooftops. The smell of roasted chestnuts and mince, of gingerbread and sugared almonds.

And everyone seemed to be in love.

It was most vexatious.

After she'd finished her errands for Mrs Bates, Mira had an hour left to do some shopping on her own. She'd searched the shop windows and remained in front of a shop that sold dolls and other playthings. There was a dainty little doll's house, and exquisite porcelain dolls in lace dresses, with china heads, hands and feet, and thick sausage curls peeking out from under their bonnets.

Clare would love it, Mira had thought wistfully.

But it was far too expensive.

She would not be able to pay the private detective his monthly fee and buy a present with the money she could set aside this month. It would have to be one of the two.

She chewed her lower lip, deep in thought. Then, with a final decision, she entered the shop and bought a bag of marbles.

It would have to do.

Next time, she had said to the doll.

"Mira!" The voice broke through her thoughts. "Where is that girl?"

"Coming, my lady!" Mira pulled herself up on the balustrade she'd been polishing, supporting her aching back with one hand and leaning back until she felt better.

My Lady, Will You Dance?

Mrs Holt was in the hallway pacing the carpet thin and wringing her hands. "Quick, to the drawing room. Lady Cullpepper wants you."

Mira straightened her cap before entering.

Lady Cullpepper was a lady in her prime; she was a buxom lady with fine blonde hair showing the first slight signs of grey. She had a nervous disposition, and there was always an air of restlessness about her. Despite occasional bouts of pettiness and demanding expectations, she had a benevolent regard for her household staff. Remarkably, she was unwavering in her commitment to keeping her promises. Seven years earlier, in a rare act of compassion, she'd offered Mira employment even though she knew she had a child; a circumstance that many other potential employers would have considered a hindrance.

"There she is." Lady Cullpepper grabbed Mira's arm and pulled her towards the window. "Stand here so I can get a better look at you." She examined Mira critically from top to bottom. "Yes, you will do."

Miss Cullpepper, a young lady in her early twenties with her mother's fine blonde hair, looked up from her embroidery. "But Mama, is it not better that I just stay at home? Really, I don't mind at all."

"Out of the question. How often do you receive an invitation to the opera from Lady Randolph?"

Rose pulled a face. "Never?"

"Precisely. So when Lady Randolph saw you at the Winthorpe dinner the other night and took such an instantaneous liking to you that she invited you to the opera tonight, you cannot refuse. You must go. It is a shame that your father and I cannot attend because we have one of those tedious political suppers he insists on. And now that Jenny has fallen ill, what are we to do? On top of your abigail and another maid, I hear. The whole household will fall ill at this rate. Oh! My nerves!" Lady Cullpepper dropped onto the sofa with a groan.

Miss Cullpepper turned to Mira with a grimace. "It seems you must accompany me to the opera tonight because Jenny, my companion, has fallen ill. It will be a dreadful affair with screeching sopranos and a stifling house full of people and no air." She shuddered. "It's quite unbearable. I usually start to feel quite uncomfortable ten minutes after entering a crowded house, and then what am I to do?"

"That's why you need an escort to prevent that. And since both Jenny and Renata are unwell, Mira will have to go instead."

The opera? Her? Tonight? Mira's head spun. "But my lady, wouldn't Emma be a better choice?"

"Emma can't possibly go. I need her myself. This dinner is important, and I need to look my best."

Mira wrinkled her forehead in concern. "But, my lady, I am a mere maid. I have neither the breeding nor the qualifications to appear in society alongside Miss Cullpepper." The thought alone made her break into a sweat.

"Nonsense. You are one of our few servants who does not speak in that dreadful East London brogue. And dressed properly, without apron and cap, I dare say you look quite fetching. You're prettier than Emma, and at the opera, appearance is all that counts."

Mira remained silent.

"I shall recompense you handsomely," Lady Cullpepper said. "I have always been generous, have I not?"

She had been. She owed it to Lady Cullpepper that she hadn't ended up on the streets. Any extra remuneration on top of her meagre wages was welcome. With the extra money she could not only pay the detective, but also buy the doll for Clare.

Mira relented. "Very well, my lady."

Lady Cullpepper's face brightened immediately. "I knew I could count on you, Mira. You must get ready, for the performance at the opera is about to begin."

Good heavens. The opera house. This was where the high *ton* gathered to see and be seen. Music was of secondary importance. What would a girl like her even do there?

"But, my lady. I have nothing to wear."

"Take one of Rose's old dresses. You have two hours to make it fit."

"But, my lady..."

"But, Mama..." Rose said at the same time.

"Hush!" Lady Cullpepper turned to her daughter. "You know you must be there, after your disastrous performance last week. Be grateful that Lady Randolph took pity on you and invited you. She has her own box at the opera, and you will meet all the important lords and ladies there. And mind you, no fainting this time!"

Rose looked like she was about to burst into tears. "It's not like I can control it. And I didn't want to faint at the ball last week."

Lady Cullpepper turned to Mira. "Mira. I implore

you. You have worked in this house for the past seven years and have proven yourself reliable. For tonight only, you are not a maid, but Rose's companion. The entire *ton* will be assembled, and the Prince Regent himself will appear. You must behave accordingly. You must pretend to be a lady."

"I'll do my best, my lady."

"Keep your eyes averted. Don't stare. Don't say anything a lady wouldn't say." Lady Cullpepper paced up and down as she lectured. "No, the best thing is to say nothing at all. Don't attract unnecessary attention. Walk straight with your chin up, as if you were carrying an invisible book on your head. Why, oh, why can't we have more time to train you?"

Mira swallowed as Lady Cullpepper's nervousness began to spread to her.

"Show me your fingernails."

Mira held out her hands.

Lady Cullpepper stared at them and slapped them away. "Terrible. You need to clean them better and cream them to make them soft. Nothing gives away your status as a housemaid as easily as your hands. I shall give you gloves. Wear them."

"Yes, my lady."

"Always remember that you are a lady of genteel birth. When people approach you and speak to you, smile with your lips closed and nod. You will always be one step behind Rose, making sure she has enough air by fanning her and having the Hartshorn salt ready. You must hold it in your hand at all times and push it under her nose as soon as she becomes pale. You will sit behind

My Lady, Will You Dance?

Rose in Lady Randolph's box. Make sure she is seen. She is healthy, beautiful, and available. She. Must. Not. Faint. Is that understood?"

Lady Cullpepper dug her sharp nails into Mira's upper arm.

"Yes, my lady. I'll do my best, my lady."

"But Mama!" Miss Cullpepper wailed. "I don't want to be available!"

"Hush, child. What on earth are you saying? Of course you want to be available and marry a handsome lord. There, there. Go to your room and get ready. Help her, Mira. Rose should wear the apple-green dress. It will suit her very well. You should wear the lavender one. Take the matching scarf and gloves. Emma will help you with your disastrous hair. And for God's sake, take that cap off!"

"Yes, my lady. Very good, my lady."

Chapter Three

The Haymarket Opera House was teeming with people.

Everyone claimed to be there to see Angelica Catalani's phenomenal performance in Mozart's *The Marriage of Figaro*. The truth, of course, was that the gentlemen of the *ton* wanted to show off their new waistcoats, and the ladies of fashion their stylish gowns. Gallant gentlemen visited the ladies in the boxes and courted them in the gallery. One flirted with fans and batted their eyelashes. One made note of whom to call on next morning and whom to send a bouquet of flowers. Thus, the opera house became a stage for amorous performances of its own, where hearts entwined, and new matches emerged.

Mira swallowed nervously and clutched Miss Cullpepper's arm for support.

"You don't need to grab me that tightly," she informed her, "I don't feel unwell yet. I'll let you know when I do."

"Yes, miss," Mira replied, loosening her grip. She clutched her reticule instead, which contained a vinaigrette of smelling salts. She feared that she might need these for herself rather than for Miss Cullpepper.

Remember, you're a lady, she repeated.

Head up. Chin up. Small steps. Graceful movements. Smile with closed lips.

Heavens! It was difficult to remember all that.

She nearly tumbled into Miss Cullpepper, who came to a full stop.

"We have to go up there now." Her voice wavered as she pointed to the marble stairs leading up to the boxes. "Lady Randolph looks impatient already." Lady Randolph had walked ahead of them, almost losing them in the crowd. She was a tall, haughty-looking woman who walked around with her lorgnette raised to her eyes.

"I'm doing this for your mother, mind you," she'd said as the carriage arrived at the opera. "To repay a favour. I have agreed to help you find a suitable match. All you have to do is sit in my box, smile and look pretty. The opera will do the rest."

"Like a piece of meat on display for the highest bidder," Mira had muttered to herself as Lady Randolph stepped out of the carriage.

Miss Cullpepper had stared at Mira, eyes wide.

Mira had smiled back. "Everything will be fine, miss."

Mira was wearing a simple lavender dress that Rose had long since outgrown. She did not know it, but she looked lovely in it, fragile and delicate.

Her hands were damp in the gloves. Why did she have to wear these things? They itched and kept slipping down her elbows. Mira kept pulling them up, wishing she could just take them off. But Lady Cullpepper had insisted that she wear them.

All the lords and ladies of the *ton* were here, each personage greater than the last. They were all wearing gloves, Mira noticed. Even the gentlemen.

They were terrifying people, names that she'd only heard mentioned through the grapevine of servants or read about in the papers. At best she would see a lofty lord climb into his curricle outside his club in Brook Street, and she would only know that because someone in the street mentioned it: "Look, it's the Earl of Buckingham!" Or she would see Lady so-and-so entering a dressmaker's shop in Bond Street, one she would never dare venture into herself. That was most of her contact with the beau monde.

Mira had no great fondness for the aristocracy. As a maid, she was invisible to them. They would never tolerate her presence or consider her a human being. Granted, the Cullpepper household had been different. Lord Cullpepper never demanded that the housemaids turn to face the wall when they met one of the family members in the corridor, and he even knew all their names and how much they earned. Lady Cullpepper was generous with gifts, knowing that it was a way of inspiring loyalty in her staff. In times like these, it was difficult to recruit and retain good servants. In that regard, their household was unusual.

In all other aspects, however, Mira's impression of the Quality had not been good, and that was not only because she cleaned up after them. The majority cared little for those beneath them, only chasing after their own pleasures. They cared only about appearances, exploiting people, taking what they wanted, and squandering exorbitant fortunes on gambling.

"I don't think I can do this," Miss Cullpepper whispered as she looked at the crowd pushing up the stairs.

Mira took her hand and squeezed it. "Yes you can, miss."

"There's not enough air in there and the walls are trying to close in on me." Miss Cullpepper was pale, and her lips trembled. They hadn't been in the opera house for more than a few minutes. Mira's mind raced.

"Close your eyes."

"What?"

Mira grabbed the girl's elbow and brought her head close to her ear. "Close your eyes, miss. And hold on to my arm. Now imagine that you are standing on a cliff, with the sea below you. Are you doing this?"

Miss Cullpepper nodded.

"The sea is so vast that it has no horizon. Can you hear the waves crashing against the rocks?" Mira moved her gently forward.

"Yes. Yes, I think I can."

"The seagulls squawk as they fly and dive into the waves." Slowly, step by step, Mira manoeuvred Miss Cullpepper through the crowded foyer and up the stairs where Lady Randolph was waiting for them in front of the box, tapping her foot and tugging impatiently at her Kashmiri shawl. A huge feather bobbed from her head.

"We've arrived. It is not far to our box, so look down and hold onto the image of the blue sea and concentrate on the music."

Miss Cullpepper's colour had improved.

"Here is Lady Randolph. Open your eyes."

"There you are. What is this dawdling? Here is our box. Sit down, sit down. Miss Cullpepper, you in front, and you in the back." There were two chairs side by side in the first row of the narrow box, and two chairs behind them. Lady Randolph sat in the left one, pointing to the one beside her.

Miss Cullpepper sat down.

Mira sat behind her, looking around in awe.

How splendid it was! The auditorium had four tiers, three with gilded boxes with allegorical figures painted in oil on the front, and the fourth was a gallery with more boxes on each side. The high domed ceiling depicted Apollo and the muses, while the gilt sconces attached next to the balustrade illuminated the entire place.

Lady Randolph raised her lorgnette. "I see everyone is here. Witherington on the right." She nodded to a gentleman in the next box. "Ignore him," she said to Miss Cullpepper. "He's a dandy and makes moon eyes at all the ladies. Not a penny in his pocket. Lady Babington on the left." She nodded to a stout lady sitting in a box beside them. The lady nodded back and continued to fan her face. "All those young bucks strutting around at the back of the gallery. Nothing useful there. Let's see who else is here. Hmm. Mr Remington is a bachelor. Ah. A tulip, but deep in the pocket. The Duchess of Newcastle. A bit out of your league, but if we could get her attention and manage to talk to her, she could introduce you to her nephew, the Viscount Dallington..."

On and on she went. Lady Randolph knew everyone

by name, their status, and the size of their fortune. Suddenly she interrupted her monologue and raised her lorgnette.

"Good heavens, Atherton is here! I did not expect to see him so early. I suppose the rumours must be true and he is here for that Catalani woman..." She caught herself and cleared her throat. She began to fan herself. "Forget my words. My point is, he's not an eligible *parti* for you as it is. Far out of your league. He is also a terrible rake. Do not, under any circumstances, look in his direction."

"I don't even know where he is or what he looks like," Miss Cullpepper muttered under her breath. Her breathing had picked up again.

"Remember, ocean waves." Mira leaned forward and murmured into her ears.

Miss Cullpepper grabbed her hand and squeezed it.

Then the music began.

Even though Lady Randolph chattered on and on throughout the entire first act, Mira was entranced. She'd never heard such glorious music in her life. The lead soprano, Angelica Catalani, sang with a crystal-clear voice, hitting all the high notes in the right places.

"Like an angel," Mira breathed. "That's what heaven must sound like."

Lady Randolph sniffed. "Balderdash. She's no angel, she's a hussy. That woman sings only for him. Shameless, the way she flirts with him on the open stage."

"Who does she mean?" Miss Cullpepper turned to ask Mira in a whisper.

"I really wouldn't know, miss." Mira didn't care either. All she knew was that this was glorious, and she just wanted to listen to the music. She could hardly remember the last time she had felt so happy.

Sometime later, Miss Cullpepper leaned back and gasped, "Mira."

She got out of her chair abruptly, and before Mira could react, Miss Cullpepper stumbled and fell backwards between the chairs with a resounding crash. It was so loud that the lead tenor, who was on his knees in front of the lady he was wooing, looked up at her, startled.

Mira jumped out of her chair, knocking it over with another resounding crash. She whipped out the vinaigrette and tripped over the chair as she tried to reach Miss Cullpepper on the floor.

"For heaven's sake, if you have to faint, do it discreetly." Lady Randolph continued fanning herself as if nothing was wrong, a painful smile plastered on her face.

Mira adjusted her head on the floor, then summoned a footman.

After a while, Miss Cullpepper regained consciousness. "I'm fine," she murmured, "just let me stay here for a while. The high balcony makes me dizzy, and there is not enough air."

"Stop this commotion at once and sit down," Lady Randolph hissed, pulling at Mira's skirt.

"But, my lady, Miss Cullpepper—"

Lady Randolph grabbed Mira's wrist and pushed her into Miss Cullpepper's seat.

"Sit here quietly, lift your chin and smile as if nothing has happened," Lady Randolph snapped. "The whole house is watching."

With a sick feeling in her stomach, Mira realised she was right.

From Miss Cullpepper's seat, Mira could see not only the entire stage and auditorium, but all the boxes as well. But that meant that everyone could see her, in turn. It was like being exhibited in a shop window on Bond Street. Several hundred lorgnettes were fixed on her. There were whispers.

Whatever was happening in her box was clearly more interesting than what was happening on stage.

Heat shot through her entire body, and she wanted nothing more than to jump up and run away, but Lady Randolph's claw had pinned her to her seat.

Mira raised her free hand in greeting.

Lady Randolph groaned. "Now the girl goes on behaving like the Queen. Ignore them all and look neither left nor right, just at the stage. Do you hear me?"

"Yes, my lady."

Mira forgot all the faces and concentrated on the music. But then, when the soprano sang a hauntingly wistful song about her lost love, of past times that had disappeared like a wisp, together with his promise made by deceptive lips with such aching sadness and yearning, it pierced her soul.

She was oblivious to the entire house watching her and how irresistibly fragile and enchanting she appeared as she leaned across the balustrade. A curl of dark hair escaped against her delicate swan-like neck, and tears streamed down her cheeks.

The *ton*, unaccustomed to such honest and innocent displays of emotion, was enraptured.

My Lady, Will You Dance?

By the intermission, Miss Cullpepper was feeling better.

"Thank heavens you're back, I feared the worst," Lady Randolph proclaimed as if the worst hadn't already happened. "There, sit, sit, sit, sit." She pushed Miss Cullpepper into the seat Mira had vacated. "And for heaven's sake, smile! Act as if nothing out of the ordinary has happened and everything will be fine. It is to be hoped this hasn't turned you into a social pariah with the commotion you've caused."

Mira and Miss Cullpepper looked at each other anxiously. What would Lady Cullpepper say? She would surely lose her position now, for she had failed spectacularly. And the entire opera had witnessed it.

The curtains had hardly fallen when the onslaught began.

"Lady Randolph. An introduction. I beg you!"

"Move back, scoundrel, I was here first."

"Nonsense, I was first. An introduction, if you please?"

"My lady! You will remember me from the ball the other night. May I meet your charges?"

"Lady Randolph! Let me get you and your lovely ladies some refreshment! You must be parched!"

"Good gracious!" Lady Randolph looked alarmed at the sounds of scuffling outside her door. "I was expecting one or two, three at the most, gentlemen to show some interest, but 'pon my soul! You've attracted the entire gamut. It appears your fainting spell did the trick. Cleverly done. Now pull yourself together, child."

Miss Cullpepper stared at Lady Randolph wide-eyed and with slightly parted lips.

"Take a big breath, miss, and just think of the sea," Mira advised, happy to retreat into the background.

But when the door finally opened, it was not a gentleman who entered, but a lady. She was tall and imposing, glittering in silver from head to toe.

For a second, even Lady Randolph looked as if the wind had been taken out of her sails.

"Lady Randolph, I presume?" The lady nodded at them graciously. She seemed even more magnificent than the Queen herself.

Lady Randolph quickly collected herself and placed her hand over her heart. "What an honour."

"I think I saw you at the ball last week. Where was it again? Ah, yes. The Witheringtons. A dull affair." She waved her hand. "This opera here is proving much more amusing. Introduce me to your lovely charges."

"Certainly. This is Miss Rose Cullpepper. She is the daughter of Lord and Lady Cullpepper, both very dear friends of mine."

Miss Cullpepper curtsied.

"A true English rose indeed. I am enchanted. How is it that you keep such lovely flowers hidden, Lady Randolph?"

"This is Miss Cullpepper's first Season, and she has not had much opportunity to appear in society."

The lady smiled. "That must be remedied. And ... this? Why do you hide in the shadows? Come forward so I can see you clearly."

Mira repressed a wince as she found both ladies looking at her.

Lady Randolph made an impatient gesture with her hand to motion her forward. Mira did so.

To her alarm, the woman stepped towards her as well until she was standing directly in front of her. She saw the diamonds of a tiara sparkling in her hair.

"This is Miss Cullpepper's companion," Lady Randolph said.

"Mira," Miss Cullpepper put in, somewhat at a loss for she did not know Mira's surname.

"Just Mira?" The lady looked amused.

"I believe she's related to the Cullpeppers, are you not?" Lady Randolph said. Mira would be a poor relative who now served as Miss Cullpepper's companion. This was the official story they'd agreed upon.

The lady reached out and took Mira by the chin, lifting her face and studying it intently. "Miss Mira Cullpepper?"

Mira held her breath and stared back into the silvery steel eyes. "No, my lady. Mirabel Taylor," she said. "But I am called Mira."

"Mirabel," the lady said quietly. "How old are you, Miss Taylor?"

"Almost six-and-twenty."

"Six-and-twenty. How surprising. There's nothing about your lovely appearance that doesn't suggest you're no longer in the first flush of youth."

Mira flushed.

"Tell me, where are you from?"

This was beginning to feel like an interrogation.

"Fowey, my lady," Mira replied, confused by the lady's piercing eyes.

"Fowey. And that would be where, exactly?"

"In Cornwall."

"Ah." The lady suddenly dropped her hands and looked at her for a moment in silence, as if considering something. Then she smiled. "Charming. How very charming." She turned to Lady Randolph. "Not one, but two lovely flowers. Rose and Mirabel. Hidden away in the shadow. For shame! I expect to see more of you in the future." She waved her hand at them. "Expect an invitation soon. In the meantime, I shall send away that abominable crowd in front of your door, yes?"

As if on command, both Miss Cullpepper and Mira fell into a curtsy.

After she left, Lady Randolph dropped into her chair with a moan. "Where's the vinaigrette?"

Mira handed her the smelling salts.

Lady Randolph sniffed them and shook her head. "Unbelievable. Truly, unbelievable. If I hadn't seen it with my own eyes..."

"I don't understand, Lady Randolph," Miss Cullpepper finally spoke up. "Who is she? She was awfully intimidating."

Lady Randolph dropped the vinaigrette and opened her eyes. "Never tell me you haven't heard of Princess Florentina? She is an Austrian princess, related to the Esterhazy family, and an important patron. Some say she wields more power than Princess Esterhazy herself. From what I've seen, I wouldn't be surprised if that were the case."

Miss Cullpepper looked at Mira with wide, panicked eyes. Mira lifted her shoulders in response.

"I suppose this is a good thing, my lady, that she has come?" Miss Cullpepper clutched her fan.

Lady Randolph looked at her with a speculative gleam in her eyes. "It depends on how you look at it. Few people know she has connections with the de Lacey family."

"De Lacey?"

"You should know the name. It is one of the oldest and proudest in England. The present head of the family is Lord Christopher de Lacey, 12th Marquess of Atherton. She is his godmother. It is no coincidence that she has come. Congratulations, Miss Cullpepper. Within the past hour, you have not only managed to charm the entire *ton*, but it appears you have also caught Atherton's eye."

Chapter Four

"This is good, isn't it?" Miss Cullpepper wailed as Mira helped her into the nightgown. "Tell me it's a good thing!"

"Of course it is, miss. The marquess is the catch of the Season, and if he's thrown an eye at you, that can only mean—" *that all and sundry knows that he can't mean anything respectable at all, aside from your silly mother, who wants to barter in her daughter for a title and fortune,* Mira nearly said, but she bit her lip. "This can only mean that you charmed him when you fainted at the opera, and that he is very interested in making your acquaintance. He may even make you an offer."

Mira vigorously brushed Miss Cullpepper's fine blonde hair.

Miss Cullpepper looked at her with wide, fearful eyes. "But they say he is so cold!"

"Well." Mira thought for one moment. "It could just be a rumour. Why not reserve judgement until you actually meet the man?"

"Mira, I shall die of fright if I ever meet him!" Miss Cullpepper exclaimed. "I shall run away and hide! And then Mama will be terribly vexed with me because she very much wants me to marry the marquess, and if not him, then some other fancy l-l-lord." Her face crumpled.

"Oh dear." Mira set her brush aside, pulled out a handkerchief and handed it to Miss Cullpepper, who volubly wept into it.

She watched her silently for a while, then shook her head.

"Very well, miss." Mira led her to the bed and sat on it next to her. "It's time for some honest talk."

Miss Cullpepper continued to sniff into the handkerchief. Mira pulled the handkerchief away and met her wet but sullen eyes.

"First of all, we both know that you do not suffer from fainting spells. You're as fit as a fiddle, if not fitter. But you are an excellent actress."

Miss Cullpepper sniffed. "You are an impertinent creature, Mira. I do not know why I allow you to speak to me like that."

"You have fooled everyone, including your mother. But not me. I believe you have been overdoing it. Extricating yourself out of undesirable social situations through fainting may work once or twice, but to the extent as you did it at the opera?" Mira shook her head in disapproval. "It won't do. You see, you only achieved the opposite of what you wanted. All the attention was on you, and now the invitations are flooding in for a delicate, frail wisp of a girl in need of protection. Men find that irresistible. I declare, if you keep fainting like that, you'll have Wellington himself worshipping at your feet."

Miss Cullpepper continued to sniff into her handkerchief. "But I don't want Wellington! And I shall have you dismissed for being saucy," she declared, then belied her words by throwing her arms around Mira and weeping into her neck. "Oh, Mira. What shall I do? I don't care about any of them. I only want my Tim!" And she burst into tears again.

Mira sighed as she patted the girl on the back.

It certainly was a tangle of sorts.

Miss Cullpepper had fallen head over heels in love with Timothy Parker, a young barrister. And while he seemed to be a decent sort of fellow, who, in turn, seemed to worship Miss Cullpepper, he had not a penny to his name. Woe to all if Lady Cullpepper ever found out.

"How certain are you that you love him?" Mira was convinced that once one of the Exquisites entered the scene and swept Miss Cullpepper off her feet, she would not waste a second thought on poor Timothy Parker. "Can it be youthful infatuation?"

"How can you even ask that?" Miss Cullpepper crumpled her handkerchief and threw it at Mira. "I love him with all my heart and soul! He wants to marry me, but as he is still at the beginning of his career, he says his income is not yet sufficient to support a family. He asked me to wait for him. I'll do so gladly. In fact, I'll do anything he asks of me. I'll be faithful to him until I die. Mama can't know because she wants me to marry the marquess." Her lips trembled.

"Well then." Mira crossed her arms. "Let me put it

another way. How certain are you that this Timothy Parker is truly deserving of this sentiment and that he loves you equally well?"

Miss Cullpepper flared her nostrils. "I just know!" She clenched her hand into a fist and pounded it against her chest. "I know here! Only someone who has never been in love can talk like you."

"Well, I would make sure that it really is love. It might be a fleeting sentiment."

"I can see clearly that you have never been in love yourself," Miss Cullpepper snapped.

Mira's face froze, then she stood up and picked up the dress, shawl and hairbrush from the floor with mechanical movements. "It is just that I do not believe in love the way you do. I do not want you to waste your youth away waiting, forevermore waiting for someone who might turn out to be—not worthy. I don't want you to get hurt, miss. That is all."

Miss Cullpepper shook her head. "I'll never understand how one cannot believe in true love. Go now, for this discussion has made me feel peevish."

"Very well, miss." Mira curtsied and left the room with a sigh.

LADY CULLPEPPER WAS OVERJOYED, for the unthinkable had happened.

Her daughter, fragile and beautiful, had conquered the hearts of the *ton* by fainting in the middle of an opera, causing even the lead tenor to interrupt his aria to look up at them in concern. The director of the opera had appeared in person in the box, anxiously inquiring after Miss Cullpepper's health.

And then the bouquets came flooding in.

"Princess Florentina came to see you in person!" Lady Cullpepper sank into a chair, and Mira rushed away to fetch another set of smelling salts, the other having long since run out. "This is beyond my wildest dreams."

That evening, Lady Randolph came sailing into the Cullpepper parlour, triumphantly waving a cream card with gold lettering.

"I knew it would happen! What did I say, Amelia?"

Lady Cullpepper snatched the card from her and perused it. "Oh dear! My eyes do not deceive me? Can this be real? Rose? Rose! Where is that girl? Call Mira too."

Mira and Miss Cullpepper entered the drawing room, both wary of what was to come.

Lady Cullpepper breathed heavily then was so overcome with emotion that she was unable to say anything. Lady Randolph took the card.

"A personal invitation from Princess Florentina to a Christmas house party at Highcourt Abbey. I am to bring Miss Rose Cullpepper and her companion, Miss Mirabel Taylor." Now it was Lady Randolph's turn to be overcome with emotion.

"Highcourt Abbey. Where is that?" asked Miss Cullpepper timidly.

"In Shropshire."

"Oh dear," Mira breathed.

"Oh my," Miss Cullpepper said simultaneously.

"Oh my, indeed. It is Atherton's residence. It seems, Amelia, that your wishes are about to come true."

Later, after Lady Randolph had left and Lady Cullpepper was getting ready for bed, she called for Mira. "Mira, you will go with Rose to Highcourt Abbey. You must never leave her side. Not until she has found a husband and is married."

"But, my lady, that's not possible," Mira said, immediately thinking of little Clare.

"What do you mean, not possible? It is not only possible, it is absolutely necessary." Lady Cullpepper slammed the hairbrush on the dressing table.

"But I'm in service. I am a mere maid, not a lady. How dare I mingle with polite society?"

Lady Cullpepper stepped up to Mira with flashing eyes. "For some reason I do not understand myself, the princess has taken a liking to you and insists that you come. You will go with Rose. You will be her companion."

Mira shook her head violently.

"What would it take for you to do as I say?" Lady Cullpepper cried. "A year's wage?"

She stilled. An entire year's wage in return for accompanying Miss Cullpepper to the country house party? She'd earned pitifully little with the Cullpeppers, but a year's wage would allow her to leave service. They could all go back to Fowey, she and Clare and Miss Pearson. They could rent a small cottage, and they could rebuild the little village school where Miss Pearson had taught so long ago. It was such a wonderful idea that for a moment Mira was breathless at the sheer magnitude of the idea.

Lady Cullpepper paced the room and wrung her

hands.

"Two."

Lady Cullpepper paused.

Mira took a deep breath. "Two years' wage and a release from service with a positive character." Mira's nails bit into her palms as she curled them into fists.

"Impudent girl!" Lady Cullpepper cried. "You're taking advantage of Rose's precarious situation."

"With respect, my lady, I am not. I simply have no desire whatsoever to go there, deceiving the Quality into thinking I am someone I am not. It's not my place, and it's not in my interest."

"Disobliging girl!" Lady Cullpepper fumed. "I don't know why I put up with you."

Mira mentally prepared to pack her bags.

Lady Cullpepper paced the room. "You are resorting to bribery and blackmail, for you know very well that if you do not go, neither can Rose. But very well. I shall give you what you want on the condition that Rose is engaged to the marquess by the end of the party."

"Your Ladyship, we both know that is highly unlikely." Mira stepped towards the door.

"Oh, very well!" Lady Cullpepper cried, after she'd paced and raged some more. "It doesn't have to be the marquess. It can be with any lord, provided he has a title and a fortune. I want her engaged by the end of the party."

Mira paused.

Two years' wages and a release from service with a positive reference.

She turned to Lady Cullpepper. "Very well. I'll do it."

Chapter Five

Their elegant carriage gracefully glided through a picturesque landscape of gently rolling hills powdered by snow. After it drove around a curve, a quaint little village with thatched cottages appeared. The roofs were adorned with a dusting of white, and the chimneys emitted welcoming tendrils of smoke. In the heart of the village stood a church, its age-old tower soaring above the surrounding trees. The sheer quaintness of the scene brought forth an involuntary smile to Mira's lips. As their carriage continued its journey, a group of village children spotted their luxurious coaches and, with unbridled enthusiasm, began to run alongside them. Touched by their innocence and the heartwarming sight, Mira couldn't help but return their cheerful waves with a bright smile.

Miss Cullpepper and Lady Randolph, both sound asleep, missed this first sight of Althorne Village.

How Mira had missed the sounds, smells, and sights

of the countryside. After all, it seemed it had been a good decision to come, she concluded.

She lowered the window and breathed in the clean, crisp, cold air.

A small wistful smile crossed her face as she heard the rhythmic sound of hammering on metal, and she glanced out of the window to catch a glimpse of the blacksmith's shop.

Under a four-columned canopy with a thatched roof stood a massive forge, the heat of which Mira could feel all the way to the carriage. In front of it, with his back to her, the blacksmith worked. He raised a heavily muscled arm to hammer on the anvil in a rhythmic pattern. His back was turned to her, and his hair was curled at the nape of his neck. With his huge shoulders, his muscles flexing, he brought the hammer down with a clank, clank, clank.

With a sudden sharp inhale, Mira gripped the edge of the window with both hands.

She watched as he lifted his arm to inspect the horseshoe he'd been working on, sinews taut and glistening with sweat, and lowered it into a bucket of cold water. It hissed.

As the carriage passed, she leaned her head out of the window to catch a last glimpse of the blacksmith, who'd turned so she could see his profile.

A proud nose and sensual, full lips.

Mira felt all her breath knocked out of her body.

"It can't be," she gasped.

She leaned further out to catch another glimpse, but

the coach was already rounding the bend to enter the curving lane that led to Highcourt Abbey.

Her head spun; her heart pounded.

It was just a trick of the imagination.

It must be.

Mira took a deep breath, leaned back in her seat and willed her heart to slow.

How often she'd seen Kit, in a random man's walk, a gesture, a laugh. It had given her a jolt every time. A jolt that shot through her like lightning and then vanished just as quickly, leaving her trembling and shaking with emptiness and disappointment.

She'd even made herself a fool more than once, following a complete stranger down entire Oxford Street, only to realise he wasn't Kit. Just because of the way he walked and the way his hair had fallen over his forehead ... this time would be no different.

When would her mind finally cease creating these illusions?

As her breathing resumed its normal pattern and her heart slowed, Miss Cullpepper stirred in her seat.

"It's cold," she complained.

Mira closed the window.

Suddenly alert, Miss Cullpepper sat up. "Look, Mira. We're approaching Highcourt Abbey. I vow I have never been so nervous!"

Highcourt Abbey was beyond anything Mira had ever seen in her life. As their carriage drove along the sweeping alley, the massive manor appeared, throning on top of a hill in the middle of a sweeping parkland surrounded by lawns and trees. As the rays of the setting winter sun fell upon the building, it glistened like gold.

"Oh my," Miss Cullpepper gasped. "This is no mansion. It's a palace out of a fairy tale."

Mira agreed but felt queasy.

Attending the opera was one thing, but a fortnight in the company of the high aristocracy, with her pretending to be a lady?

How could that go well?

Surely, they would see through her quickly, that she was no lady, but a fraud.

Would they throw her into the Tower when they discovered who she really was? Would they clap her into Newgate?

"The good thing about this place is that it is expansive," Miss Cullpepper mused. "I like the wide, open lawns with the lakes at the front. There will be space to breathe. And the house itself seems to have sufficient space. It won't crowd me in, will it? And surely it is big enough for all the guests to get lost in. With a bit of luck, it won't be as cramped as those London townhouses, and I won't feel faint all the time."

"Surely not, miss." Mira's stomach somersaulted.

Lady Randolph awoke with a short snore just as their carriage pulled into the court. "Have we arrived already? 'Pon my soul, if it isn't the princess waiting at the entrance."

With another lurch in her stomach, Mira saw the erect figure of Princess Florentina standing by the Corinthian columns that framed the entrance. Next to her stood a line of servants, the butler, the housekeeper, footmen and maids. As if on command, they all either bowed or curtsied as they exited the carriage.

Lady Randolph almost dropped her lorgnette. "Goodness me, what a reception!"

It was the first time that Mira was being greeted by the servants, not standing with them. She always stood in line like this when the Cullpeppers returned from a journey.

Her hands were sweating as she stepped out of the coach.

"My dears, it is such a pleasure to have you here," the princess said languidly. Mira curtsied impulsively, which was the right thing to do, for Miss Cullpepper did the same.

"Atherton sends his regrets that he cannot be here to greet you in person, as he has pressing matters to attend to. You will join him for dinner. His Grace, the Duke of Aldingbourne, has just arrived, along with his sister, Lady Evangeline, and Count Lindenstein. The rest of the guests will be arriving next week for the ball."

Lady Randolph looked astonished. "Are you saying, Princess, that this is to be a more intimate gathering?"

"Precisely, my dear. Precisely. The crowd will arrive for the Christmas ball, so let us enjoy the solitude until then."

Lady Randolph looked overcome at having been singled out for such an exclusive invitation.

"I fear that with Atherton, Aldingbourne, and Lindenstein forming the formidable trio, there will be more politicking than I care for. It will be very dull. But with you here, we will keep them in check, yes? Together with Lady Evangeline, the three of you will be the ornaments of the party, which would otherwise be a dead bore," the princess said.

"Ornaments like Greek vases on the mantelpiece," Mira muttered to herself after the Princess turned away.

The princess turned suddenly with a twinkle in her eye. "Not vases, but flowers, mind you. Flowers."

Goodness, she'd heard her! Mira hastily averted her eyes with a flush. The princess had hearing like a lynx.

THE MOST CHALLENGING thing for Mira in her new role as a lady was to do nothing at all. She had to clasp her hands tightly together to keep herself from inadvertently joining the hustle and bustle of the servants around her. Unpacking trunks, sorting clothes, fetching buckets of water, arranging the linen, dusting the chest of drawers. But this was not what a lady did.

A lady, Mira discovered, spent a lot of time dressing and undressing. Not only that, but she had to stand around while others dressed and undressed her. More than once she had to resist pulling away as a maid helped her pull up her stockings, pull her dress over her head and fasten it. Not to mention allowing her to do her hair.

"Under no circumstances must anyone discover that you are not a lady," Lady Cullpepper had insisted repeatedly. "It will reflect badly on Rose."

So her identity was that of an impoverished distant relative, a cousin of sorts, a companion to the daughter of the house.

It was a difficult position.

My Lady, Will You Dance?

With a growing sense of unease, she thought of the suppers and soirees they were expecting in the coming days. How on earth was she going to get through them?

She pushed the feeling away.

Her job here was to see to that Miss Cullpepper found a husband.

Anyone would do, provided they had a title and a fortune.

The sooner she accomplished that, the sooner she could return to Fowey.

Chapter Six

Teatime was intimidating to say the least.

Mira was sitting in the most beautiful drawing room she'd ever seen, surrounded by the high aristocracy, drinking tea like a lady.

She took care to sit up straight on a chaise longue, sticking out her little finger as she lifted the delicate teacup, just as she'd seen ladies do. She took a tiny sip and set the cup down again.

There. That was good, was it not?

It wasn't as if she was completely incapable of lady-like behaviour. After all, Miss Pearson had taught her not only reading, writing and arithmetic, but also etiquette, elocution, and posture. She could almost hear her voice instructing, "Tuck in your elbows. Sit up straight. Stomach in. Bosom out. No arms on the table. No slurping. No chewing with your mouth open. And, for God's sake, always speak slowly and clearly."

She'd taught Mira the King's English with such

perfect pronunciation that she'd become an oddity in the village.

"Mira is putting on airs," the other children said. "She thinks she's better than us because she doesn't talk like us."

And they wouldn't let her play.

When Miss Pearson found her sprawled on the grass, sobbing, she'd sat down beside her with a sigh. "I know it's hard," she'd said. "But one day, child, you will thank me for this."

Mira stared blindly at her teacup.

Miss Pearson had been right.

She thanked the heavens now for all that Miss Pearson had taught her, however useless she'd thought it all to be at the time. She must have had some kind of uncanny premonition that Mira would one day find herself in such a situation. If it hadn't been for Miss Pearson, she wouldn't have known how to behave at all now.

Mira's stomach rumbled, but she dared not eat the tiny triangle of a cucumber sandwich that lay before her on a plate.

Her courage was failing her miserably.

The problem was not that she did not trust herself to do so in a ladylike manner.

The problem was that everyone in the room was looking at her.

She straightened her skirt and brushed an invisible crumb from her lap.

She took the napkin from her lap, inadvertently used it to rub the top of the mahogany table as she was wont to do when polishing the tabletop, then caught herself and dropped it as if it were a piece of glowing ember.

For heaven's sake, she was a lady, not a maid!

It was better to do nothing at all.

So for the next few minutes, she stared intently at the Greek vase on the small side table beside her.

She dared to raise her eyes and came to the momentous conclusion that she was definitely not imagining things.

They were all watching her.

The Duke of Aldingbourne, a terrifyingly austere-looking creature, sat morosely in a corner, arms and legs crossed, looking at her broodingly.

A blonde-haired gentleman with a German aristocratic name she'd already forgotten, looking like a fallen Apollo with a decadent kind of beauty, sprawled in an armchair nearby. He studied her, the tip of his finger tracing his full upper lip thoughtfully, as if she were some sort of puzzle. She tore her eyes away from him with a flush.

Then there was Princess Florentina, sitting across from her, observing her with unbridled amusement. Did she just wink at her?

Maybe I have a crumb stuck on my lips, Mira thought, and licked her lips, only to remember that that couldn't be the case, as she hadn't eaten anything.

Miss Cullpepper looked at her helplessly, with her usual timid demeanour. Surely, she too was out of her depth in this elevated society.

Mira hoped that Miss Cullpepper would faint so that she would have an excuse to leave the room. But when it came down to it, her condition remained vexatiously sturdy.

The most perplexing stare was that of Lady Evangeline, the Duke of Aldingbourne's sister. She sat next to Mira, rather close, uncomfortably close, and she kept edging even closer.

Mira wanted to move away, but if she moved an inch to the right, she'd fall off the chaise longue.

Lady Evangeline leaned into her and pushed her face up to hers, with eyes that seemed too big in her narrow elfin face and a mouth that was too wide.

Mira leaned back as far as she could, gripping the edge of the chaise longue to keep from falling off.

Lady Evangeline grinned, revealing a set of charmingly crooked teeth.

Zounds! They knew she was a fraud.

The aristocracy couldn't be deceived. They knew she was a mere housemaid. They could sense it. It was in their blood. Any time, any one of them would call her a hoax and pounce on her, and then she'd be dragged off to Newgate.

Mira clenched her sweaty hands into fists and waited for the axe to fall.

But no one said anything.

Even Lady Randolph, usually so voluble, was speechless in the presence of so much high nobility.

The clock was ticking.

Someone ought to say something? Whatever it was that they normally discussed at teatime.

Even she, a lowly housemaid, could tell that something was not quite right about this situation.

For heaven's sake!

If they were about to call her out already and have

her thrown in Newgate, let it be done and over with already. Because this was simply unbearable. Unbearable!

Completely unnerved, she cleared her throat. "Lovely weather today, is it not?"

The duke's frown deepened.

A corner of Apollo's lip curled upwards.

Miss Cullpepper looked at her in surprise.

The princess raised an eyebrow.

All heads turned now to watch the soggy sleet slide down the windowpane.

Mira almost sagged in relief. At least they were no longer looking at her.

But she found that it only lasted a few seconds, for the duke's head snapped back almost immediately to resume his forbidding stare.

Lady Evangeline emitted a gurgle of delighted laughter. "You are so right! Fabulous weather, indeed!"

She jumped up and down in her seat, grabbed both Mira's hands in hers, and beamed, leaving Mira entirely flummoxed.

What on earth was she so happy about?

"Miss Taylor."

Mira jumped at the duke's dark, deep tone.

"Pray tell us where you are from."

"F-Fowey, Your Grace."

"And that would be where, precisely?"

"South Cornwall, Your Grace." Mira knit her forehead together anxiously. The conversation was almost identical to the one she'd had with Princess Florentina at the opera.

"And you would be how old?"

It *was* identical, the interrogation.

She licked her lips. "Six-and-twenty, Your Grace."

Lady Evangeline nodded as if she'd given the correct answer to an arithmetic question.

"Fowey. That would be the little farming village on the west coast near St Ives," the duke observed.

Mira shook her head. "No, sir. It's a harbour town on the east coast near St Austell."

"Ah yes." He lifted a pale hand. "There is a small Gothic church on the edge of town with an interesting relic in it. I forgot the name."

"Do you mean the Church of St Fimbarrus, Your Grace? If so, it is in the centre of the town and there is no relic. It is of Norman origin."

"Is it now?" His dark gaze remained intently on her face. "You may be right."

Mira shifted uncomfortably and looked away.

"And how long has it been since you were last in Fowey?" he continued.

"About seven years, Your Grace."

He lifted a finger. "So you moved from Fowey to London seven years ago. You were nineteen." He drew an invisible line in the air from one point to the other.

"Yes, Your Grace."

"Why?"

Mira stared at him. "Because I, err—" *I couldn't find a position as a governess, try as I might. No one would take me on because I had neither character nor references but a child. Lady Cullpepper was the only one willing to hire me as a housemaid.* She nearly blurted out the whole story, then bit her tongue at the last minute. "Because..." What on earth was she supposed to say? She wasn't prepared for this. She had no idea what to reply.

"Because my mother asked Mira to be my companion." Miss Cullpepper spoke up unexpectedly.

Mira gave her a grateful look.

The duke raised an eyebrow. "Did she, now?"

Mira began to knead the dress in her lap and looked away. "Yes, Your Grace."

"Hmm." He curled his fingers. He seemed unconvinced.

Lady Evangeline took Mira's hand in hers and patted it. "Yes, and now you're here, and I think it's fabulous. Tell me one thing, Miss Taylor," she moved to sit even closer to her, with a confidential air, "you must believe in the nature of true love, do you not?"

Princess Florentina clucked.

Apollo, who'd followed the conversation sleepily, seemed to wake up.

"Evie," the duke growled.

Mira looked at her, baffled. "I beg your pardon?"

"Do you believe in true love?" She tilted her head to the side and gripped Mira's hands.

Miss Cullpepper laughed suddenly. "We just had that conversation, didn't we, Mira? Alas, I am chagrined to report that she does not."

Lady Evangeline's face fell. "You don't? But you must! Whyever would you not?"

"Evie!" The duke frowned. "Behave. Remember what we agreed upon before."

"Yes, Julius. But Miss Taylor, why? You must tell me why."

"I confess I'm rather curious about the answer to that particular question as well," Apollo sat up, leaning his elbows on his knees and looking at her with interest.

Mira looked from one to the other, wondering if they'd all gone mad. But perhaps this was the natural behaviour of the aristocracy. She wouldn't know.

To buy some time, Mira lifted her cup to drink what was left of her cold tea.

When she looked up, she found the duke watching her. Again.

She supposed she'd get used to being stared at eventually.

"Because I am not a romantic. I am a realist, and I know that life is not all cream and roses, and that it is better lived not on the affections of others, but on one's own efforts alone. I don't see the point in wasting one's life waiting for a love that may never come."

Lady Evangeline perked up at once. "Oh, but what if..."

"Evie," the duke thundered, causing Mira to spill some tea onto her lap. "Drop this inappropriate topic instantly."

Lady Evangline sat back, sulking.

The duke crossed his arms and returned to his morose stare.

Apollo murmured, "Fascinating."

She must have imagined the brief look of sympathy that flashed through his eyes before he sank back into his armchair.

My Lady, Will You Dance?

Lady Evangeline jumped up with a huff, walked up and down, then exclaimed, "How tiresome that Atherton is not here. Really. He invites us all to a Christmas house party and then he's not even here to greet us."

"Indeed," said Lady Randolph, polishing her lorgnette. "We haven't set our eyes on the master of the house yet."

"Well, we all know that when it comes to manners and etiquette, Atherton isn't cut from the usual cloth," Princess Florentina said dryly. "He has been called away on unexpected business and will join us shortly."

Lady Evangeline walked over to the window, pushed the curtain aside, and looked out. "Well, I suppose we all know he has no manners. That's what I like about him, although he can be awfully cutting and cold. Somehow, things always become interesting as soon as he enters the room." Her glance wandered over to Mira again and she gave a decided smirk. "He's irresistible anyhow. You'll see."

Well, wonderful. Next to the terrifying duke interrogating her, and the decadent tulip assessing her, she'd have to deal with a cold marquess without manners.

Suddenly, Lady Evangeline emitted a shriek, startling Apollo out of his semi-sleep. "He's here! He's here! How exciting!"

Indeed, the sound of horses' hooves and the crunch of wheels on the gravel came through the window.

Inexplicably, Mira's heartbeat quickened.

Miss Cullpepper looked faint, and this time, it did not look as though she feigned it.

There was only so much Mira could take. "If I may be

excused." She jumped to her feet. "I need to change my dress as I've spilled some tea on it."

Miss Cullpepper looked relieved. "Me too. I'll join you."

"Yes, yes, freshen yourselves and change into something more appropriate for dinner. Then you can meet the marquess." Lady Randolph looked indulgently at Miss Cullpepper. "Put on something pretty, child."

"The child has unexpectedly well-bred manners, considering her background," Princess Florentina remarked to no one in particular after the girls had left.

"Miss Cullpepper has had only the best governesses," Lady Randolph piped up.

"Hm. I did not mean Miss Cullpepper. She is somewhat of the timid sort, is she not? But prettily behaved as well."

"It's all very puzzling," Miss Cullpepper said on the way up to their rooms, "how everyone is so singularly focused on you. Not that I mind, for that considerably lessens the burden on me, and I much prefer to watch from the sidelines. But their behaviour has been excessively odd."

Mira exhaled a shaky breath. "It was, wasn't it? I thought I'd imagined things. What do you think the reason might be? Do you think they've discovered that I'm not really your companion?"

Miss Cullpepper tilted her head aside thoughtfully. "I thought you did rather well, Mira. Lady Evangeline didn't behave nearly as well as you. I am not certain, but

My Lady, Will You Dance?

it could be, of course, that they are merely trifling with you. Also, you must stop calling me Miss Cullpepper. I am just Rose to you. I must say I prefer it anyway. We shall be friends, yes?"

Mira gladly agreed.

They arrived in front of Rose's room, which was on the first floor. It was a pretty, medium-sized guest room in blue, with a walnut chest of drawers, a little desk in the corner, a washstand, and a comfortable bed.

"It's a shame they didn't give me a room next to yours," Mira said. "Surely this place is not lacking in guest rooms. Now I have to walk a mile to reach your room to assist you."

Rose frowned. "Another one of those odd things. Show me your room."

Mira had been given a room in a completely different wing. When she'd stood in it earlier, she'd gasped.

The room was yellow and gold, papered with delightful Chinese wallpaper, and the entire front of the windows looked out onto the main lawn of the house. She had the fountain and the lake at her feet. It was an astonishing sight. Her bedroom had a flight of four adjoining rooms: a morning room, a dressing room and, most charming of all, a lovely little connecting room with a mahogany desk, a small sofa, and a bookshelf full of books. These were rooms fit for a queen.

"It's somewhat big for a guest room, is it not?" Mira asked doubtfully.

Rose's hand travelled over the fine damask of the bedspread. "This is not a guest room," she said slowly. "It looks like one of the master bedrooms." She walked over to the door, but it was locked. "I wonder whether this is the connecting door to the master's room."

She turned to Mira, her eyes wide. "We've got it all terribly, terribly wrong!"

"What do you mean?"

She raised a hand and pointed a finger at her. "It's not me he wants. It's you."

MIRA WANTED nothing to do with any of this.

The strange people, the even stranger house.

Never mind the money. Never mind Rose, who'd clung to her, begging her to stay.

She'd saved enough to take a mail coach. She was going home.

Mira had thrown on her coat and was trying to tie her bonnet as she hurried down the broad staircase and out into the street.

She would have to follow the drive until she reached the great arched gateway a few miles from here, for it was a vast estate. She'd go to the little village, and surely it would be possible to catch a coach from the inn.

Mira marched along the drive, muttering, "Crazy people."

Of course, after Rose had mentioned it, it all came together.

The opera.

Rose fainting, and Mira taking her seat in the front.

Princess Florentina appearing in her box.

The invitation.

It had been for her, not Rose.

It was a bit strange, though, that the marquess would use Princess Florentina to catch his lady loves. But who knew, maybe this too was one of the peculiar ways of the nobles these days.

It must be some kind of strange game they were playing, in which they were all complicit. Much like hunting prey. It was cruel, and altogether evil.

Well, she would not play. She would rather roast in Hades than be seduced by a nobleman and become his mistress.

Master bedroom with a connecting door, indeed!

Mira sniffed.

She stepped into a puddle of cold sleet and felt the water seep into her thin boots.

The gate was still a long way off. To the left was another, narrower path leading off to the side.

Beyond it were the outbuildings, stables, and coach houses.

Surely there was another way out of the huge estate that did not cut through the main park, for the servants needed to be able to get in and out quickly.

A carriage stood outside the stables, horses neighing.

Set apart from them was a red brick cottage with an adjoining workshop.

The workshop they'd passed earlier.

A man stood with his back to them, lifting a horse's foot as he worked to apply a new horseshoe. He was tall and muscular, and despite the cold, he wore a shirt that was rolled up, revealing flexed muscles.

Mira stopped in her tracks.

Suddenly time stood still. All sound fell away.

She watched him set down the horse's foot and straighten up.

There was something familiar about his figure.

A cold, numbing sensation spread through her body as the blood drained from her face.

As if sensing her presence, he turned slowly, and their eyes met.

Chapter Seven

SEEMINGLY OUT OF NOWHERE, HE WAS THERE.

Taller, older than before.

The slim, boyish frame had filled out and become brawny and broad on top. The hair was the same thick and forevermore tousled, falling into his eyes.

His eyes. Mud brown tinged with green.

Mira drew in a ragged breath.

"Kit."

Her legs buckled under her, and she collapsed in the middle of the gravelled, soggy driveway.

He was with her in an instant.

"Mira. Dear sweet Lord. Mira."

HE CARRIED her into the workshop, wrapped her in a blanket, and rubbed her hands.

Repeated her name over and over again. "Mira." And then, "You're in shock."

Was she?

She couldn't feel a thing. The numbness still had her whole body in its grip, and the iciness in her veins had a firm, icy, numbing grip on her heart.

She felt dizzy and lightheaded. Her mind reeled with disbelief.

"It feels cold," she said through chattering teeth.

"Here, something hot." He pressed a hot mug into her hands. "Drink."

But she could not swallow; the paralysis had taken hold of her whole body. She dropped the mug.

"Kit," she whispered. "Are you really here?"

He crouched beside her, a troubled, unreadable look in his eyes. "Yes, Mira."

"All this time? You've been here?" She couldn't believe it. She licked her dry lips before she said, "Not d-dead in a ditch, or swinging at Tyburn, or shipped off to the colonies." Her breathing became shallow and quick. "You were here all the time. S-safe."

"Yes."

She stared at him. "I see."

She wrapped her arms around her knees. She was still shivering.

He reached out to touch her face, but she pulled away. He froze, then dropped his hand.

He got up, stoked the fire in the stove, and eventually the heat penetrated, the chattering stopped, and some coherent thoughts began to form in her mind.

"All the time. You were here."

She glanced around, taking in the earthen floor, the forge, the anvil, the tub of water next to it, and the various tools lying about. "This is your forge?"

"Yes."

"Does he pay you well? The marquess, I mean."

His head snapped up.

"Of course he does, what a silly thing to say. He must pay very well," she said tonelessly. "The cottage attached here must be yours, too."

"Yes." It came out as a whisper.

"It's a very nice cottage, and big. Much bigger and better than what could ever be had in F-Fowey."

"Mira—"

I will build you a little cottage with my own hands...

She blindly picked up the mug from the floor, wiped it on her skirt and placed it on a small wooden table. "So you left to get yourself a better position as a blacksmith in this grand place. You are a master now."

At first it seemed he would not answer. His face was turned away.

How strange that she felt nothing at all. Only numbness and tiredness seeping into every inch of her body.

"I'm staying at the manor," she told him. "As Miss Cullpepper's companion. She has been invited to his Lordship's party. I am forced to spend more time with the nobles than I care for, but it pays well. They are very snobbish and very strange. The duke is awful, the Austrian count is a terrible flirt, and I haven't even met the marquess yet. I am supposed to behave like a lady, which I often forget. Sometimes I catch myself in the nick of time, just as I'm about to clear the table or dust the chest of drawers. It's a hard habit to break."

She babbled.

He nodded woodenly. "Are they treating you well?"

"Well enough."

She got up, untangled herself from the blanket, and dropped it to the floor. She pressed the back of her hand to her forehead and closed her eyes.

When she opened them again, her eyes took some time to focus on him.

"Why?" she whispered.

He tensed immediately.

"Why, Kit? *Why?*"

She stepped up to him and pushed against his chest, causing him to drop the hammer and stumble backward against the anvil. His arms hung at his sides, and he did not defend himself. Nor did he answer.

She hammered at him. "Why. Why. Why?" It came out as a scream.

"I—oh God, Mira, what can I even say?" he whispered brokenly.

Mira dropped her hands.

He stood before her, his head hanging, defeated.

She felt the coldness envelop her again and welcomed it. She withdrew deep into it, for it numbed something that could be pain.

She did not want to feel it.

"You are right. There are no words. For some things, there simply are no words." She drew in a shuddering breath. "You're alive. You're doing well. That is good. That is something one must be grateful for. I suppose… that's all that really matters." She turned to leave the shed.

"Where are you going?"

"I must return to the house before my absence is

noticed," she said tonelessly. She'd completely forgotten about leaving.

He stepped up to her and took her icy hand in his. "We need to talk," he urged.

She supposed they should. It was what would be expected in a situation like this. But her mind refused to cooperate.

They had been so close, once. There had been a time when they could almost read each other's minds.

But now there was a gulf between them that was bigger than the chasm between the earth and the moon.

It was unbearable.

"I want to—I have to go now. Please." She pulled her hand away.

"You're still in shock. Tomorrow. I will come to the house tomorrow. Then we'll talk."

She nodded, turned, and walked unsteadily back to the manor. She did not turn to see Kit standing there, watching her go with an expression on his face that was heartbreaking.

MIRA EXCUSED herself from dinner and all other entertainment for the evening, claiming to have a headache.

It wasn't even a lie. Her head was throbbing wildly and her breathing still hadn't returned to normal.

"You look like you've seen a ghost. You aren't about to fall ill, are you?" demanded Lady Randolph. "Not so close to Christmas."

"Oh, you must not fall ill, Mira." Rose had accompanied her to her room. "There are the Christmas festivities coming up, and the ball, and it will be frightfully splendid, and I shall be absolutely terrified without you. I am sure I will faint with fright again. What shall I do if you are indisposed and can't attend any of it?"

"I shall be fine. I suppose all I need is some rest."

Then, alone in her huge room, a feeling of panic overcame her.

Perhaps none of it had happened?

Had her mind played tricks on her?

Maybe he'd been a figment of her imagination?

Maybe he'd left again?

Hands unpicked her clothes. She'd been bathed, a maid had brought up a lavish tray of food, and then she'd been tucked into the massive yellow bed, which had been pre-warmed.

She'd finally found Kit, after seven long agonising years.

But he was no longer her Kit. He was a stranger.

And now she wished it had only been a dream.

In her dreams she was back in Fowey, the Fowey of her childhood. She'd lived with Miss Pearson, who'd taken her in after her parents died and taught her reading and elocution.

"You must learn well so that one day you can take over the village school," she had preached every day.

"Yes, Miss Pearson," she'd replied, and after she'd done her chores, she ran wild over the meadow high over the cliffs, where the waves crashed into the rocks. She swam in the freezing sea and picked shells on the beach and watched the sand squish between her toes.

No matter the weather.

Then, one day, when returning after such an excursion, her wet hair slapping into her face, she passed the cemetery.

A boy was standing in front of a freshly dug grave. His tattered clothes hung from his lanky frame, and he bowed his head as the coffin was lowered into the grave.

"That's his mother, God rest her soul," muttered Farmer Smith, who was unloading his cart. "One of the kindest, gentlest ladies that ever walked the face of the earth. A real lady, they say. She was of good stock. The world did her much wrong."

"Why did she die?" Mira asked. She could not tear her eyes from the boy's defeated form.

"Typhoid."

"And the boy?" Mira asked.

"Kit. A right 'un, that one. Nursed his sick mother to the end. Dirt poor they were, too. Did all manner of work about town to earn money for the doctor and medicine. Has nobody left in this world now." Farmer Smith sighed and walked on.

Mira went home slowly, her thoughts heavy with illness and death.

She could see the graveyard from the kitchen window as she sat down to eat with Miss Pearson.

The boy was still standing by the grave, his head hanging. When it started to rain, he still stood there, motionless, as if he did not feel the rain.

When it got dark, she saw his dark silhouette still by the grave.

Mira looked at the plates of biscuits on the table. She took some, wrapped them in newspaper, picked up the lantern and left the cottage.

The boy looked like half a spectre himself, standing so immobile at the graveyard. She shivered.

She set down the lantern by the grave, unwrapped the biscuits, and wordlessly held them out to him.

He did not respond at first.

Mira crouched next to him, trying to peek up into his face. Strands of his long, dark hair hung over his forehead.

Just as she was about to give up and walk away, he lifted his eyes.

Mud-green they were, full of despair.

His eyes fell on the biscuits she was still holding out. His hand moved slowly to take them.

Mira gave him a wavering smile, left the lantern by the grave and went home.

A few hours later she heard Miss Pearson exclaim, "Dear sweet heavens, if that boy didn't give me a fright." She pointed out of the window.

He was standing by the garden gate, in the pouring rain.

"What's he doing here?" When she'd heard Miss Pearson's startled cry, Mira had jumped out of bed and run down, barefoot.

"Probably doesn't know where to go, poor mite." Miss Pearson sighed. She opened the door. "Well, don't just stand there, boy. Come on in, then."

He slept in a little cot by the kitchen hearth and took care of odds and ends in the household.

"I saved you, didn't I?" Mira told him one day as they walked across the meadow to pick berries.

He tugged at one of her wild corkscrew curls. "So you did, my Mira."

Soon after, he began an apprenticeship with Master Williams, the village blacksmith. He moved out of Miss Pearson's cottage to live in the forge. But every spare minute he had, he spent with Mira.

"First I'll be an apprentice," he'd explained to Mira. "Then a journeyman. And then I can become a master myself. And then, when I have saved lots of money, I shall build a cottage for us. With my own hands. I'll marry and take care of you, Mira. And I'll look after Miss Pearson, too."

"That'll be very nice, Kit." She'd beamed at him.

She'd been ten and he was thirteen.

She'd loved him fiercely ever since.

Chapter Eight

THE LADIES WERE GATHERED IN THE BREAKFAST room while the gentlemen set off for an early morning hunt.

"That is something I'll gladly let them do on their own," Lady Evangeline put in, shuddering, for it was cold and dark outside. The ladies had risen early to see the gentlemen off, but Princess Florentina insisted that it was the first and last time they'd do so, for she didn't see why everyone had to rise at an ungodly hour simply because the men insisted on hunting.

"It was worth catching a glimpse of them in their hunting gear," Lady Evangeline grinned. "They cut a fine figure, I must say."

Mira had missed all that. After a sleepless night of tossing and turning, she'd fallen asleep at dawn and risen late.

As soon as she stepped into the breakfast room, Lady Evangeline, in her usual effervescent manner, jumped up from her seat and took her by both hands, exclaiming that she was so relieved that Mira was feeling better, though it was a shame she'd missed seeing the gentlemen off, and how handsome they all looked in their hunting clothes.

"We missed you yesterday, but I dare say you needed some time alone to rest. Come and sit down, I'll bring you a plate." She piled a plate with scrambled eggs, kedgeree, beans, and bacon and placed it in front of Mira. "There. You look awfully pale. You must eat."

Mira thanked her and picked at the food.

"Atherton didn't make an appearance until dinnertime last night," Lady Randolph said. "I was beginning to think we'd never see his face again. And my, what a mood the man was in! He was dreadfully surly and aloof the entire evening."

"That's usual for him. He's much like Aldingbourne," Lady Evangeline put in cheerfully. "That's why they get on so well, you see. They're two of a kind. They've been friends for a long time, you know."

"Are they really two of a kind?" asked Lady Randolph. "Methinks where Aldingbourne might come across as somewhat morose, Atherton is, as they say, cold. In Aldingbourne's case, it is entirely understandable, due to the early loss of his wife. They say he never got over her death. But in the case of the marquess, there is an impenetrable barrier that surrounds him that leaves one quite baffled. They call him the Cold Marquess for a reason. There is no better way to put it."

"I agree with your assessment," Lady Evangeline said. "Underneath all this moroseness, Aldingbourne is a soft, cuddly bear. I daresay it must be the same with Atherton. I have known him for a while, and he does thaw somewhat in more intimate company. One needs to crack the shell to reach the real man."

Lady Randolph shook her head. "I beg to differ. If one ever manages to crack the marquess' ice shell, I daresay one would find even more ice underneath."

"I suppose he was simply tired from a long day," Lady Evie added thoughtfully, "But it's true; he doesn't smile, ever." She shrugged. "But neither does Aldingbourne."

"And then there was Lindenstein, who oozed charm and good nature and charisma to make up for everyone else's remiss. The man never stopped smiling, not even when he was eating." Lady Randolph shook her head, baffled. "He managed to flirt with Lady Evangeline, Miss Cullpepper and me simultaneously. What a rake!"

Lindenstein. That was the blond Apollo's name.

"In short, it was a good thing you missed supper last night," Rose muttered to Mira, who had barely paid attention and found herself unable to swallow as much as a morsel. "I'll take a leaf out of your book and try to do the same tonight: retire early."

The ghost of a smile flitted across Mira's pale face. "Was it that bad?"

"It was terrible! The marquess addressed me in front of everyone. I thought I would faint, but this time for real. And of course I was terribly tongue-tied and could do nothing but stammer nonsense. To which he simply smiled." Rose shivered. "What Lady Evangeline says about him never smiling isn't true at all. He does smile. But it is a mocking, sarcastic kind of smile that cuts you to shreds. I died on the spot."

"That sounds terrible indeed." Mira couldn't help but feel relieved that she'd missed dinner.

Rose leaned against her, her blonde curls touching Mira's dark ones. "And I was right too," she murmured. "About what I said yesterday. He isn't interested in me in the least. He couldn't even recall my name! Instead, he enquired about you."

"Did he, now?" Mira found that this left her entirely indifferent.

"He asked in a rather flinty way as to where you were. '"Miss Taylor?"' He raised an eyebrow like this." Rose tried to raise one eyebrow but failed and raised both. "And when Lady Randolph said you were unwell and had retired early, he said in this frightfully stern manner, 'I shall not have any of my guests missing dinner,' and then he turned to the footman behind him and had a tray sent up to you." She paused thoughtfully. "I suppose one could say that was unexpectedly considerate of him. Which makes me think I was right. He must have seen you at the opera and is certainly interested in you. Yet, he is a marquess, and you my companion. You must be careful, for he can't mean anything honourable by it. I am very worried about you, Mira. Make sure the doors are firmly locked at night."

Mira sighed. "Why on earth would this man be interested in me? There are dozens of other willing women he could have. I haven't even met him."

"Which makes it all the more intriguing." Rose shrugged. "At the same time, I'm relieved. I shall attempt to enjoy the festivities and the ball as much as I can, and then return to my Tim. I miss him so. But Mira, you must try to avoid the marquess at all costs."

She nodded. "I shall feel unwell in the evenings and miss all the social entertainment. But it is bound to be difficult with the upcoming festivities. I shall have to fall very ill to miss all that."

It wasn't a bad idea. That would give her time to seek out Kit. They still had much to discuss. She hadn't even told him half of it.

Her heart lurched at the mere thought.

"What on earth are you thinking, Miss Taylor? You've buttered both sides of your toast." Princess Florentina shook her head.

"I'm afraid I'm somewhat scatterbrained today," Mira said. "My thoughts seem to be all over the place."

"I recommend you cease thinking altogether. Too much thinking is not good for a lady," Lady Randolph observed.

Lady Evangeline jumped up and ran to the window. "Look! It's snowing!" She clapped her hands. "How marvellous!"

Indeed, thick snowflakes were falling from the sky, powdering the landscape.

"We must make snowmen and snow angels, and skate on the lake when it freezes over. And, oh! We have not collected any greenery yet. We must hang mistletoe everywhere! It will be a fabulous Christmas this year. Miss Taylor, tell me, how do you celebrate Christmas in Cornwall?"

The question brought up a pang of wistfulness.

Christmas in Cornwall had always been magical. "We have pasties and fairings and stargazy cakes," Mira told her. "There is guise dancing during the twelve days of Christmas, with mummers singing and dancing on Montol Eve as they move from door to door in return for money and food."

"Disguises and stargazing? What on earth could that be?" Lady Randolph wondered.

"Fairings are ginger biscuits, and stargazy pie is a fish pie. It has the heads of pilchards peeking out of the pastry," Mira explained.

"To have fish eyes looking at you out of the pie! Not my idea of Christmas." Lady Randolph pulled a horrified face.

"It may sound odd, but it is what I grew up with back in Cornwall."

Kit used to buy her fairings as gifts at the Launceston fairs, because it was customary for men to buy the gingerbread biscuits with sugared almonds for their sweethearts. They were delicious and Mira would always associate them with Kit. But Kit had always claimed that her homemade biscuits were better. At Christmas time she and Miss Pearson baked up a storm of sugar biscuits, not only for themselves but also for their pupils and their families. These had been special biscuits in the shape of a snowflake. Kit had designed and made the biscuit cutter himself, so they were the only biscuits of this particular shape in all of Cornwall...

"I do prefer some proper English wassail, mince pie, and Christmas cake," Lady Randolph proclaimed.

"We shall have to collect greenery, and hang up some

mistletoe," Lady Evangeline said and clapped her hands. "Let that be our plan for today."

Mira thought it was a good plan. If they were to be outside the entire day gathering holly, ivy, mistletoe, and fir branches, she would surely be able to find an opportunity to slip away and find Kit.

Chapter Nine

THE OPPORTUNITY AROSE WHEN LADY EVANGELINE and Rose went into the woods to gather mistletoe. To their delight, there was plenty of mistletoe hanging from the trees.

"I could kick myself a thousand times," cried Lady Evangeline, "for forgetting that we need a ladder and shears. One of us needs to go back and ask for a footman to help us, for the gentlemen, who are grossly neglecting us in this endeavour, are nowhere in sight. Fie!"

Mira offered to return to the house. She informed a footman of the exact location of Lady Evangeline and Rose, with a request for assistance. She waited a moment for the footman to leave, then made her way to the outbuildings.

Her heart hammered irregularly at the thought of seeing Kit again.

Yet the smithy was empty. The fire in the forge was cold, and there was no sign of anyone working in the workshop.

She knocked on the door of the blacksmith cottage, but no one opened, either.

Wondering where else to look, she wandered around the buildings to the stables, where there was much activity, with grooms and stable hands rushing about to tend to the massive stallions that stood huffing and steaming in the yard.

It appeared the men had just returned from the hunt.

Mira ducked behind a stable door just in time to hear the sound of swift footsteps and Aldingbourne's deep voice, "I dare say the deer will be easier to track in the deep snow." Another voice, probably Lindenstein's, uttered some sort of reply.

She waited a moment for them to pass, then made her way carefully around the back of the building, pausing at the entrance to a small, empty stable. Just as she was about to return to the smithy, a hand shot out of the open door, clasped around her mouth, and pulled her into an empty stall.

Her first instinct was to bite, struggle, and kick, then she felt herself being pulled against a hard chest. An old, familiar smell of leather, smoke, and heated iron filled her nose.

"What in blazes? You scared the living daylights out of me," Mira gasped as the hand fell from her mouth.

"I'm sorry I frightened you. But I didn't want anyone to see you. I did not expect to run into you here, since I intended to go to the house to find you." Kit reluctantly loosened his grip but kept his hands on her shoulders as they faced each other.

The closeness disconcerted Mira. The man standing

before her was so familiar, yet not. He was dressed in shirtsleeves and an apron covered his leather breeches. A lock of dark hair fell across his forehead, and his eyes were fixed intently on her.

She shifted her gaze. "I did not want to wait any longer. I looked for you at the forge, but you weren't there."

"His Lordship's stallion lost a shoe, so I was called to the stables." He dropped his hands and stepped away.

"So this is what you do here. Fixing his Lordship's horseshoes."

"Among a host of other things. They use me as a jack of all trades."

He picked up a wooden stool, set it upright for her to sit on, then looked around for another. There was a tiny wood-burning stove used by the stable hands to warm their drinks.

Mira watched as Kit lit a fire in the stove. Then he picked up the other stool and placed it next to hers, leaning his elbows on his knees, his gaze fixed on the fire.

Silence fell between them.

"Talk to me," Mira said. "I need to know why. I need to know why you've been here all this time, obviously doing well, plying your trade, but not only that, you have become an indispensable member of this estate. And you never, not a single time, not even once, sent a message. A note, a letter, or, if writing proved too cumbersome for you, a messenger that you were alive and well. All these years. Not a single word. Why?" Her voice had risen.

"It wasn't for lack of trying..." he began, but Mira cut him off.

"Start at the beginning. That day. The morning of the fifteenth of June. I sent you to fetch eggs."

He nodded slowly, as if remembering the day.

She'd wanted to prepare pasties, with swede, potatoes, and meat inside. Succulent and delicious, they had been Kit's favourite meal. Mira loved making them, folding the ingredients into the crescent-shaped pastry dough and crimping the edges. Only that morning she'd run out of eggs, so she'd sent him to Farmer Smith.

Kit had grabbed the basket, planted a kiss on her mouth, followed by two more, and he would have stolen another if Mira hadn't pushed him out of the door, and he'd grinned and sauntered through the garden gate with a cheerful whistle on his lips.

He hadn't returned.

Mira had waited and waited for hours, certain at first that he must have been distracted. He must have met some friends or colleagues who would have summoned him to the Old Ferry Inn for a pint of ale.

When he returned, she would scold him for going to the tavern in broad daylight.

But he did not return by the afternoon.

Mira threw down her apron and went to see Farmer Smith, who confirmed that Kit had indeed picked up a dozen eggs that morning.

"But that was long before lunchtime. He must've gone to the tavern with some mates," the farmer suggested, confirming Mira's suspicion.

Mira marched into the village and headed for the Old Ferry Inn, which was on the banks of the river Fowey.

My Lady, Will You Dance?

The innkeeper denied he'd ever set foot there, nor was he in the taproom of the Old Rooster.

Kit had the day off, so he wouldn't be at the smithy, would he? Master Williams frowned when she went to ask for him.

"You know he wouldn't be here today of all days, lass," he'd said.

Mira had made her way back to the cottage, confused. The first strands of worry had begun to nag at her. She took a different path this time, not the shortcut across the meadow, but along the road. Surely he couldn't have gone into the neighbouring village? Or to the fair in St Austell to pick up fairings? He knew how much she loved them.

There, in the middle of the junction of two roads, she saw a dark object lying on the ground, amidst a sticky yellow mass.

It was the basket with broken eggs.

Mira clenched her hands as she remembered the anguish of the days that followed.

"Well?"

"I fetched eggs from Farmer Smith," he said in a faraway voice, as if remembering was difficult. "Instead of taking the shortcut across the meadow, I decided to take the road back to pick some apples from the apple trees by the road." He rubbed his hands over his thighs. "I was hoping you'd make me some sweet apple pies."

Kit had a sweet tooth, and sometimes the apple part in half a pasty wasn't enough for him. He preferred to have the whole pasty filled with the spicy apple filling.

"'Then?" Mira prompted.

"Then ... a carriage stopped. There were some gentlemen in it. They ... desperately needed a blacksmith to help with some horses they'd left by the wayside. I decided to help them. One of them in particular was pleased with my work and immediately offered me a job, only it would be away from Cornwall. I refused. He insisted. Eventually he made me an offer I couldn't resist. The condition was that I go with them on the spot. When we stopped at the next inn, I had a message sent to you. It appears you never received it."

He didn't meet her eyes.

She stared at him in disbelief. "What farrago of nonsense are you trying to dish me up? I wasn't born behind the moon." She stood and shook her head. "Who offers a random blacksmith on the road employment? Aren't there enough other blacksmiths in the country they could have asked?"

He did not meet her eyes when he said, "Ultimately, their offer turned out to be irresistible."

Mira kept shaking her head. "How entirely out of character for you to do such a thing. The Kit I knew would never, willy-nilly, have gone out on the road with complete strangers who happened to offer him work in return for leaving his whole life behind. The Kit I knew could have been offered all the riches of the world, and he would have thrown them back with a scornful laugh before he'd do such a thing to those he loved."

She glowered at his bowed head.

Then he lifted his head. "The Kit you knew, Mirabel, was a foolish, naive boy who knew nothing of the ways of the world."

"Foolish, perhaps, but never naive, and you certainly knew the ways of this world, with your difficult childhood and how you struggled and fought to provide for your poor mother. If there was one thing that defined Kit, it was loyalty. There is no person more loyal in this world." This belief in him, deep in her heart, was what had kept her going all those years.

He looked haunted.

Mira drew in a shuddering breath as the truth began to crystallise in her mind, sharp and unforgiving. "But I suppose you are right. People do change. I thought I knew you better than anyone, but I may have underestimated the discontent that must have eaten away at you over time. I always knew you wanted more. When your grand lord offered you a position here on the estate, it must have been irresistible. You took it because you saw a chance to get out of the daily grind you must have felt you were in. You felt trapped and you saw a way out. Because in the end, it wasn't quite good enough for you. The village, your job with Master Williams, the cottage." Her mouth tightened into a bitter line before she added, "Me."

His head shot up. "Mira. No. Never that." He grabbed her hands. "You cannot, must not, believe that." He said it with such savage fierceness that she almost believed him.

A great weariness overtook her.

"What else is there left to believe but that you abandoned me?" she whispered, her voice quivering with a mixture of disbelief and heartache.

His face was ashen. "No. Never. Is that what you have been thinking all this time?"

She stared at him blindly. "Why not? It happens to women all the time. I simply never thought it'd happen to me."

He pulled his hand through his hair in agony. "No. I never abandoned you. Not for one minute. Not for one second. You must not believe that. It's not as it seems. Sometimes things happen in life that are so inexplicable to the point of being absurd, it's beyond anything conceivably possible. Sometimes it's circumstances beyond our control. Sometimes things are simply not what they seem."

"Then what else should I believe, Kit? Tell me, what else is there left to believe? What else?"

He knelt in front of her and flung his arms around her and crushed her to him.

She clung to him helplessly. After a moment, she attempted to squirm out of his embrace.

"Please let me go." Her voice broke.

"Never. Now that I have finally found you, I'll never let you go." His voice was muffled.

His entire body shook.

For a moment she smelled the familiar smell of Kit.

Without thinking, she lifted her hands and cradled his face. His cheeks were wet. His face was more angular, harder, gaunt than before. Gone were the boyish, carefree laughter lines. There were new lines. A hardness about the jaw. Around his mouth, a line of suffering. Or was it bitterness? She traced it with a finger.

My Lady, Will You Dance?

He turned his head and pressed his lips into her palm.

She flinched, drew her hand away, lowered her head. Her eyes fell on his hand.

How she'd loved these hands.

The burn scar that welded itself to the back of his hand. He'd burned them when he was still an apprentice, learning to be a blacksmith.

He'd buried his mother with those hands.

Her eyes fell on the ring he wore on his finger.

She dropped his hand as if it burned her.

With these hands he'd wanted to build their own house. Brick by brick. A little house for you ... and the child.

Dear sweet heaven.

Mira drew in a shuddering breath. "Kit. There's something you need to know—"

"You *must* believe me. Whatever happened was one of those absurdities of life that you'd never believe possible, not even in your wildest dreams. What happened was that—"

"Where's that bloody blacksmith?"

A door slammed, hurried footsteps. A shout.

Kit cursed. "This is no time to talk. Later. Go. I'll find you."

She stumbled to the door.

Without looking back, she ran back to the manor.

Chapter Ten

He still wore the ring.

The thought revolved in her mind and she could not move beyond it.

The weight of her discovery pressed heavily upon Mira's heart—the fact that he still wore the ring he'd made.

Her hand instinctively crept up to her neck, where a delicate chain adorned with her own ring rested. Leaving it on her finger had proven to be impractical, for she'd had to use her hands for hard labour. When they left for Highcourt Abbey, she hadn't wanted to leave it in the box where she usually stored it but placed it on a chain and wore it around her neck instead.

Had Kit worn the ring all those years? Or had he just slipped it onto his finger moments before their unexpected reunion?

Mira hesitated; her heart conflicted. Such a gesture seemed out of character for Kit, the man she had once known so well. Yet, how much did she truly know about the man he had become over the years of separation?

She'd firmly believed every word she'd told him earlier. There wasn't a person under the sun who was more loyal than Kit. She knew that with every fibre of her soul.

But now, in the unexpected revelation that he had been living and working on this glamorous estate all along, safe and sound, Mira's world teetered on the brink of upheaval. It defied all reason and shattered her previous assumptions. Her steps faltered as she gazed vacantly into the distance, grappling with a reality that she had never dared to entertain.

It was a bitter realisation, one that implied abandonment, an act that cut deeper than she could have imagined. She couldn't fathom how everything they had shared might have been built on deceit.

Yet he'd denied it vehemently, almost savagely. And these reassurances felt so genuine.

Mira's mind wrestled with conflicting emotions.

Would he abandon her again?

What about Miss Pearson?

What about Clare?

A fierce surge of protectiveness welled within her, causing her to clench her fist in resolve. She would not allow anyone to inflict harm upon them, not even Kit, the man who had re-entered her life with a past shrouded in shadows and mysteries yet to be unveiled.

Her hand trembled as she rubbed her forehead.

A crack appeared in the numb shell that encased her heart.

My Lady, Will You Dance?

"Miss Taylor! Miss Taylor!" A breathless voice greeted her from across the field. Lady Evangeline and Rose rushed towards her, followed by several footmen, who carried piles of greenery on their arms.

Lady Evangeline carried a sprig of mistletoe. Her cheeks were red, and her eyes were sparkling.

"There you are! Where have you been? We wanted to wait for you, but then it started to snow heavier, and it got uncomfortably cold, so we decided to return, especially after we managed to find this wonderful specimen of mistletoe. What do you think?" She lifted it for Mira to examine.

"It is beautiful, and I am sure it will serve its purpose well," Mira replied woodenly.

"Yes, it will, won't it? I shall hang it over the blue parlour. Or wait, perhaps over the yellow salon. Or the ballroom door? In any case, somewhere where there will be some inevitable kissing." She smiled. "Not that I should decide these things, since I'm only a guest here, but I'm sure Princess Florentina won't mind, and Atherton is indifferent to what I do anyhow. I could hang a donkey from the ceiling of his library, and he would neither notice nor care. So perhaps over the door of the yellow drawing room, or in the middle of it. Not that I will have the opportunity to kiss anyone." She sighed dramatically. "Of the three gentlemen here, one is my brother, whom I'd rather not kiss unless I can help it, the other is suffering from a hopeless love, and the third is colder than ice and indifferent to everyone and everything. I don't care much for kissing any of those men, handsome as they are. So maybe this mistletoe is entirely superfluous? What do you think?"

"Oh! You don't say!" Rose exclaimed. "So Lindenstein is suffering from a hopeless love? And the one who is indifferent, of course, must be Atherton. He is colder than ice. I agree with that assessment. Now, tell us more about Lindenstein's hopeless love."

Lady Evangeline leaned forward, head bowed, and whispered confidentially, "Lindenstein never made a secret of it. I heard him talking about it with the other gentlemen. It is a star-crossed love. Poor man! As for Atherton, you have to wonder why he is the way he is, don't you think? Is the ice encasing a broken heart, perhaps?"

Rose's eyes widened, and Mira shrugged. She really could not be bothered with all this gossip, not when she had so many problems of her own to deal with.

"Of course, Miss Cullpepper won't need the mistletoe, she's in love with her barrister," Lady Evangeline said. "She told me all about it while we cut the holly. As for me, it does not matter who I kiss because I too am already engaged to someone else."

Both Mira and Rose stopped and looked at her, surprised.

"Yes, did you not know?" Lady Evangeline said. "I can kiss as many men under the mistletoe as I like; in the end, I shall have to marry the man who has been chosen for me. This is the fate of the duke's daughter. He is someone I have never even met," she added in a matter-of-fact voice as she marched on.

Mira shook herself, then caught up with Lady Evangeline and took her arm. "Wait. You're engaged to be married to someone, but you've never seen the man? You've never even talked to him?"

"No. He's a family friend, an Austrian count, horribly old and ugly, but there's nothing to be done about it, because our engagement has been decided since I was in my leading strings. We are to be married once this horrid war is over. You need not feel sorry for me, for even if I have to marry the old man, a grand adventure awaits me. I shall finally be able to travel and see the Continent, you know! Besides," she waved her hand, "I'm quite used to the situation, and I refuse to get morose about it. Although sometimes I can't help getting a little morose. Especially when it is Christmas and there is no one for me to kiss."

"But Lady Evangeline—" Mira began.

Lady Evangeline turned. "I wish you'd drop the title and call me Evie. Don't you think that's what best friends do, call each other by their first names? I don't have many friends, you know..." A wistful shadow flitted across her face.

"Evie, then."

"And you are Mirabel. And Rose." She beamed at them both. "Now I have not one, but two friends! I am so glad you are here! Now, where shall we put the mistletoe?"

Chapter Eleven

As the guests gathered for the country house party, Atherton's absence was conspicuous.

He hadn't joined them for tea. He didn't turn up for the afternoon's entertainment of cards and charades hosted by Evie. Nor did he turn up for the evening soiree.

It was almost as if the man was avoiding their company, yet no one commented on it.

Mira was relieved.

To be on the safe side, she excused herself again for supper, and was glad to be able to retire to her room early.

Her emotions were in turmoil. For all those long, lonely years, her unwavering belief had been that Kit couldn't have willingly abandoned her. She'd been steadfast in the conviction that he'd been taken from her by forces beyond his control. He'd been taken, he'd been kidnapped, he'd been sold into slavery, he'd been gang-pressed into the army and taken to the colonies. Any of these had seemed a plausible explanation for his mysterious disappearance. Through it all, she'd clung to the certainty of his love, the unshakable faith that he would return.

But to find him here, working as always in a smithy, alive and well, amid the opulence of this wealthy estate, caused her world to crumble around her.

It meant that he'd chosen to depart willingly.

It meant he'd abandoned her.

He'd abandoned Clare.

But he couldn't have known about Clare. He wouldn't have known, for she'd discovered she was with child only after he'd left.

Her soul was at war with herself.

Because it wasn't like him.

This simply wasn't Kit.

How could she, in the truth staring into her face, still have such unwavering faith in him?

She shook her head as if to shake away the fear and the doubt.

She knew she'd have to tell him about Clare. She'd have to tell him about this precious secret that had been her sole source of solace throughout the years of hardship.

Small rattling noises at the window made her look up sharply.

There it was again—clack! As if someone was throwing pebbles at the glass.

Mira pushed aside the curtains and looked out.

Below, on the snowy driveway, stood Kit.

She opened the window with trembling fingers.

"What are you doing there?"

"I had to see you," he said. "I had to see if you were really here and not a figment of my imagination."

"Lower your voice. They'll catch us and then you'll be thrown out, and I won't get my wages."

"Can you come down?"

"I'm in my nightdress."

"Very well, then, I shall come up."

"No. Wait. How?"

Without much ado, Kit stepped up to the wall of the manor house, grabbed a handful of ivy, put his foot on the windowsill on the ground floor and hoisted himself up.

"Goodness, be careful," Mira hissed. He pulled himself into her room and stood in front of her.

He was wearing a coarsely woven linen shirt with a waistcoat over it, knee breeches and heavy leather shoes. Mira wondered for a moment how he could climb up the wall in such heavy shoes.

He stared at her.

"What was it you wanted to say?" she asked, painfully aware that she was barefoot and wearing only a flannel nightgown, her hair tumbling loosely about her shoulders.

"I wanted to say—this." He reached out and pulled her into his arms, his mouth closing over hers.

It was the deep, passionate kiss of a drowning man.

Mira's legs buckled underneath her, but he held her tight, lifting her up and kissing her hard.

After a while they broke apart, gasping for air.

"You can't do this," Mira gasped.

"I can't do what? Kiss you?" He grabbed her again and planted another kiss on her lips. "By Jove, I have seven years of kissing to make up for."

Mira shook her head. "You can't just disappear without explanation, then suddenly reappear and—and climb into my room in the middle of the night and kiss me like nothing ever happened. It's outrageous."

"Yes, it is. Very well. I see your point." He sat down on the bed and pulled her into his lap. "You are right. We must talk. We definitely must. Talk to me."

"I..." Her thoughts were a heated jumble without head or tail—but maybe that was because he was in the process of pressing delicious little butterfly kisses up and down her neck.

"No talking? Very well," he said huskily before he proceeded to nibble at her earlobe, "then I shall just continue kissing you."

"Kit," Mira hissed, but she felt her bones melting like butter in the warm summer sun.

"We could compromise," Kit murmured, "we could kiss first, then talk..."

There was a sharp knock on the door. "Mirabel, are you asleep?"

They froze.

"Mirabel? You haven't fallen asleep yet, have you?" Evie asked. "I see the light is on under your door."

"Answer her," Kit murmured in her ear.

"I'm still awake."

"Oh famous. I'll come in then."

"No, no, no, wait!" Mira jumped up and ran, panicked, in a circle. "I'm not, er, presentable. Wait, wait!"

She grabbed Kit's arm and shoved him to the floor. "Under the bed!" she squeaked. He crawled under the bed and Mira pulled the covers over the side so he was hidden.

Then she sat on the bed and called, "I'm ready now."

Evie entered. "It was getting rather dull with you gone, and Rose retiring early too, and Atherton having to leave again. He really is the worst host ever. I tried to flirt with him a little over the pudding today, but goodness! I couldn't get a word out of him. So I was left with my grumpy brother and Lindenstein, who interests me like an orchid would."

"An orchid? How so?"

Evie sighed. "Pretty to look at, but that's about it. He's in love with someone else, remember?"

"I think you mentioned that, yes."

"It's such a sad Christmas. For me it is. For you it should be the happiest of all, shouldn't it?" She gave her a mischievous look.

"What do you mean?"

"Nothing. I was just saying. I just wanted to see how you are faring. Aldingbourne has forbidden me to talk about it, but I couldn't help noticing that you've been awfully pale these last few days. Almost as if you'd had some kind of... shock. I thought you might like to talk about it." Evie looked at her expectantly.

Mira squeaked. Not only because what Evie said had surprised her, but also because a warm hand had suddenly grabbed her foot ...

... and pressed a kiss on it.

Evie misinterpreted the squeak as agreement. "I am right, am I not?"

Mira flushed. "It is just because I have contracted some sort of head cold. Nothing to talk about, really."

She kicked her heel backwards. A muffled sound from under the bed told her she'd hit the target.

Mira coughed to cover the noise. "I seem to have developed a cough, too." She coughed harder.

Evie's face fell. "Oh. You really are ill." She stood up. "I'll send you some warm lemon water with honey. And an aniseed balm to put on your chest. I hear it works wonders."

"That's very kind of you, Evie."

"I will leave you now, but you must get well quickly, yes?"

"I'll do my best," Mira promised.

After Evie left, Kit crawled out from under the bed.

"What are you doing? She nearly discovered you."

Kit grinned. "Your foot was irresistible."

"Really." She crossed her arms. "I'm not in the mood for this."

"I see you're not. I shall cease tormenting you, then."

"Yes, you should. I am very angry with you and in no mood for silliness."

"What was it you wanted to tell me?"

"Assuming ... things had been different," she began haltingly. "Assuming something had happened, something important but entirely unexpected, completely out of your control, something that would have changed your entire life, not just yours, but mine ... forever. Would your world have still been too small? Would you still have left? Would you have made the same choices?"

He looked at her with a tilt of his head.

"Assuming things had been different," he countered. "Assuming something unexpected had happened, something important, something life changing and entirely out of your control; assuming I were no blacksmith, and I took you to a grand ball, in a grand house, would you dance with me then? And if you did, would you see me as the man you knew before? Would you treat me the same? Would you still love me the same?"

"What kind of a nonsensical question is that?" Mira whispered.

"Precisely. What kind of a nonsensical question is that?"

They stared at each other.

"Kit—" she began.

"I'd better be going. It is late, and Lady Evangeline is right, you look pale and have dark circles under your eyes. I don't want you to fall ill."

He planted a hard kiss on her lips, opened the window and swung out.

"Kit!" Mira called softly after him. She looked out and saw him sprinting across the snow-covered lawn.

She closed the window and leaned against it with a sigh.

She'd wanted to tell him about Clare.

EVIE HAD INSTRUCTED the footmen to hang the mistletoe in the middle of the room, where everyone would be standing or sitting for tea.

Kisses would be inevitable.

Lady Randolph and Princess Florentina discussed

the upcoming Christmas dinner and ball. "People will be arriving in the next few days and the house will be quite full. It will be quite amusing to see everyone scrambling to attend the Atherton Christmas Ball. It is quite a thing," Princess Florentina said.

"Oh!" Evie put down her teacup as an idea struck her. "Do you think Atherton will allow the waltz? I have heard it is such a sublime dance, but I have not had the opportunity to dance it."

Lady Randolph sniffed. "I hear it is quite a scandalous dance."

Princess Florentina looked pensive. "I have danced it, of course. There is nothing indecent about it at all if you have a partner who can dance it with verve and vigour. I suppose we could ask Lindenstein to teach it to the ladies. He's Viennese, it's in his blood. They have been dancing it for years. With your permission for Miss Cullpepper, of course."

Evie clapped her hands. "Oh yes, let's do it! Please!"

Lady Randolph nodded. "Of course I will not withhold my permission in this case. If you say it is not inappropriate, and that you have danced it yourself, I will trust your good judgement."

"Wonderful!" Both Rose and Evie were delighted with the news.

"The gentlemen will join us shortly, then we can inform Lindenstein of his inevitable fate of teaching you the waltz," Princess Florentina said.

Mira stood up. "If I may be excused? I left my embroidery in the library."

"Be sure to rejoin us shortly," Princess Florentina said.

My Lady, Will You Dance?

Mira curtsied and left, intending to lose herself in the house all afternoon and then claim to be unwell in the evening to avoid dinner. It was a shame that she would miss the dancing lessons, for she loved to dance. But there was nothing she could do about it.

She needed to stay out of everyone's way.

She walked along the corridor, crossed the foyer, and heard swift footsteps descending the stairs above her. The stairs made a clockwise turn before coming to rest directly in front of her.

"My word, Atherton, we need to discuss this hunting tactic of yours in greater detail ..."

Mira was heading for a head-on collision with the marquess and his male guests as they headed for the drawing room.

She froze. Then she panicked.

She looked around wildly, saw an inconspicuous panelled door under the stairs and dove for it. Just as the door closed behind her, she heard the men crossing the foyer.

With her heart pounding, Mira turned to find herself in the servants' staircase, which led on one side to the kitchen below and on the other to the stairs above. She decided to climb up, and after carefully opening the door, she stepped out and found herself in the great gallery.

It was a magnificent room, all pistachio green, with light streaming in from tall windows framed by brocade curtains on one side of the room, while on the other wall hung life-size portraits and oil paintings of landscapes.

Mira had never seen anything like it.

She was completely alone in the gallery.

She needed solitude. She needed to think about Kit, about what it meant that he was here. About his inability to send a message all those years. How it all made no sense at all...

She walked along the gallery, marvelling at the splendour that surrounded her. She did not know much about art, but she sensed that the works hanging here were priceless. The one she liked best was a winter scene in the Netherlands, with ice skaters on a lake.

What was it like, she wondered, to live in a place like that? Not as a maid, but as its owner. How long would one be able to appreciate the beauty of the place? Did one, after a while, take it all for granted as one developed a sense of entitlement to such riches? How long would it take to become jaded and indifferent to such worldly splendour?

Mira wandered from portrait to portrait, studying the ladies and gentlemen in Elizabethan and Baroque dresses and wigs. She found that most of them looked rather bored and jaded. There was one elderly gentleman who had a decidedly unpleasant air about him. He had a gaunt face and a cruel line around his mouth. He wore a wig and a baroque coat.

George William De Lacey, 11th Marquess of Atherton.

Surely, this couldn't be the present marquess. Atherton wasn't that old, was he? He must be the predecessor. He looked like he had been an unpleasant sort of fellow.

Mira shivered and was glad she would never have to meet him.

My Lady, Will You Dance?

She walked on, stopping in front of a small, inconspicuous landscape painting at the end of the gallery. It was easy to overlook.

It showed a deep blue sea and waves crashing against the shore. In the distance was a picturesque little harbour town.

She would recognise her hometown anywhere.

Tears welled up in her eyes. How accurate, how lovingly painted this picture was! She could almost hear the seagulls, feel the sun kissing her skin, the smell of the sea.

But how strange.

Mira's eyes wandered over the portraits in the gallery again. Most of them were heavy oils.

Then this small, insignificant painting of her Fowey.

Why of all the harbour towns... Fowey?

She stared at the gnarled yew on the cliff. It was her tree. Hers and Kit's. It was at the centre of the picture. This was where they had spent countless afternoons together. This was where he'd proposed. He'd carved their initials into the bark. No one knew the significance of the tree... except for her and Kit.

Her mind thought the unthinkable.

No.

It couldn't be.

It was impossible, utterly preposterous, utterly absurd.

Her heart pounding in her ears, Mira lifted her skirts and ran along the gallery, down the main staircase and into the red salon where the ladies were gathered.

"There you are. We were wondering where you'd

disappeared to again," Princess Florentina said, putting aside her embroidery.

"Where is he?" Mira burst out.

"Who on earth do you mean?"

"Atherton. Where is he?"

Chapter Twelve

MIRA DID NOT WAIT FOR AN ANSWER.

She turned on her heels and marched out of the room and into the hall. There she turned to the right and opened the next door. The dining room was empty.

She would open door after door in this palatial mansion until she found him.

The next room, the library. A housemaid dusted the books and jumped when she tore the doors open. Mira apologised and moved on.

Next room.

"Mirabel!" Evie had come rushing after her, followed by Rose. "What's happened? You look like you've seen a ghost."

Without answering, she marched into the next room, the blue salon, which was empty as well.

"If you're looking for the gentlemen, they've retired to..."

Mira walked out and flung open the next door.

"... the billiard room. There, you've found them."

Mira marched inside.

It was a gentlemen's room with oak panelling and a large billiard table standing in the middle. The two gentlemen who had been lounging in leather armchairs jumped to their feet.

Leaning over the billiard table was a third gentleman, impeccably dressed, the cue stick placed to make a shot.

He looked up and their eyes met.

This was when it finally cracked, the numbness that had encased her heart. Like fractured glass, it shattered into a million pieces.

She welcomed the anger, the pure, unadulterated fury that rushed through her veins.

Mira pointed a shaking finger at him. "Outside. Now, your Lordship," she spat.

"Dear me." Lindenstein muttered. "That doesn't sound too good, *mein Freund*. Don't tell me you haven't cleared the air by now...?"

Mira shot him a look that could have killed him on the spot, then turned on her heels and marched out, past an astonished Evie and Rose, both of whom had their hands clasped over their mouths.

She did not look back to see if he had followed her.

Not knowing where to go, her emotions got the better of her, and she exploded in the middle of the foyer for all to hear.

"You useless wretch! You liar! You misbegotten, chuckle-headed dolt!"

Thereupon followed a string of Cornish expletives that would have made any sailor blush.

"Mira. Mirabel. Listen to me. It's not as it appears."

Mira stared in disbelief. He dared to counter with a hackneyed argument? That really was the last straw.

"Not as it appears? That's all you have to say? All these years I have searched for you! I spent every penny I had trying to find you, I starved myself half to death to save up enough to hire a detective! Do you have any idea what it means for a single woman to be alone in London without means or money? I ended up in the workhouse, Kit, the bloody workhouse! Had it not been for Lady Cullpepper, who was willing to take me on as a housemaid, I would have ended up walking the streets. And you know what? Even then, I would have kept looking for you! These hands," she waved them in his face, "have scrubbed and worked and cleaned and toiled for the sole purpose of finding you. I was certain that something terrible had happened to you, that you had been taken against your will, when all the time you were here, sitting in this golden palace, on your golden throne, surrounded by all your glorious riches, playing the lofty marquess. And it is not as it appears? I will tell you what it is: it is beyond words, that's what it is. It is beyond anything I could ever have imagined."

Looking around wildly for something to get her hands on, she grabbed the nearest vase and hurled it to the floor. It exploded on the floor with a satisfying crash.

"My God, Mira." His face had gone grey. "The workhouse? I had no idea."

"No, you didn't, did you?" A bitter line formed around her mouth. "You're a despicable lout. You never even bothered to write or send a line."

Crash. The second vase shattered on the marble

floor. He attempted to take her arm, but she shook him off. She looked around wildly for another vase.

He picked up a celadon vase from a side table and handed it to her. "You are so right. Everything you said. I am a despicable lout. A cowardly liar. There are no excuses. I should have tried harder. I should never have believed the old devil when he said you were dead. I should have searched for you. I should have told you about all this right away; I should have approached you at the opera. Instead, I hid, and then I could not muster the courage to speak to you under any identity other than the blacksmith you have always known me as."

Mira swung the vase at him, then grabbed hold of it just before she smashed it to the ground. She narrowed her eyes. "You arranged for me to come here. You planned and schemed the whole thing like it was a game."

"Not a game. Aldingbourne insisted we had to verify your identity first. I had no doubts, but after all this time we had to make sure you were indeed Mirabel Taylor."

Mira gave him a bitter, hard stare. Then all the fight went out of her. Still clutching the vase, she went to the main entrance and out into the driveway.

"Where are you going?"

"Home." She marched down the stairs to the driveway, without coat or shawl, and in her satin slippers, which were immediately soaked as she stepped into a puddle.

He followed her.

"I'm going home to Fowey. I am done here," she told him, wiping angry tears from her cheeks. "I'm done with everything. All the empty promises and hopes and lies

My Lady, Will You Dance?

and searching and waiting, always waiting." She stumbled, then fell and sat down in the middle of the drive, clutching the vase as if her life depended on it. She burst into big, ugly sobs that racked her body.

He dropped to the ground beside her and wrapped his arms around her.

"Forgive me, Mira. Forgive me. I thought you were dead. All these years. They told me you were dead. I am sorry. I am so, so sorry."

He rocked her back and forth as they cried together, holding each other.

"Shocking. Utterly, completely shocking." The ladies were glued to the window of the drawing room, intently observing the drama unfolding outside.

"It is beyond words. Such a vulgar display of emotion! Has the world ever seen such a thing?" Lady Randolph could not move beyond her shock, but had her nose pressed to the window so as not to miss a single act of the drama. "What is he doing now?"

"He's sitting next to her and hugging her." Rose blinked hard. "They're both sitting in a puddle. He is weeping. They are both weeping."

"I wouldn't believe it if I hadn't seen it with my own eyes. Atherton, weeping. How can that be?" Lady Randolph pulled out a handkerchief and blew her nose awkwardly. "There. What did I say? That coldness of his was only a façade."

"Atherton has finally, finally found his long-lost love," Evie proclaimed, then wept loudly along without a handkerchief. Rose handed her a serviette and she blew her nose noisily. "I would be so pleased, except they both seem rather upset about it. Shouldn't they be happier?" She looked around, troubled. "It's not exactly the happy ending I envisioned. What shall we do now?"

The only person who remained unfazed was Princess Florentina. She took a pair of scissors and cut the thread. "Happy endings need time. Now the healing can finally begin."

Chapter Thirteen

THE PROBLEM WITH COUNTRY HOUSE PARTIES WAS that, regardless of the tumultuous dramas unfolding within the grand residence, etiquette had to be maintained at all costs. Guests were expected, particularly neighbouring acquaintances from the surrounding area, to arrive in ignorance about the emotional turmoil that had transpired mere minutes before their arrival.

The show of grandeur and festive merriment had to go on, for the sumptuous Christmas supper at Highcourt Abbey was a tradition steeped in both opulence and discretion, where the outside world remained blissfully unaware of the storms that brewed underneath the manor's elegant façade.

At least, this was how it had always been, until that particular evening.

THERE HAD NEVER BEEN A GLOOMIER supper.

His Lordship, the Marquess of Atherton, had done

something shockingly out of the ordinary. Instead of escorting the highest-ranking lady present to the dining room, he'd offered his arm to an unassuming girl with neither name nor breeding.

The silence in the room as he stood with his arm outstretched had been awkward and tense.

For a moment it had seemed that she was about to stick her nose up in the air, refuse his arm and storm off. But then she'd placed her fingertips on his sleeve, as if afraid she'd burn herself, and he'd led her into the dining room to her seat to his right.

It was the seat of honour.

Who was she again, this Miss Taylor? Where had she sprung from so suddenly?

And why was she sitting between the host and the Duke of Aldingbourne as if she were a person of importance?

She was a pretty girl, all right, in a simple evening gown. Some would even call her beautiful; small and fragile as she was, with dark ringlets falling around a perfect oval face and a pale pink petal mouth. She seemed unusually pale, however, with dark shadows under her eyes that made them appear even bigger.

Atherton had made no attempt to break the awkward atmosphere. He sat at the head of the table, stone-faced and silent, and ate his meal rapidly. But one was used to that, for it was well known that the marquess was aloof and unapproachable, and altogether a difficult person to converse with.

It was the ladies who saved the supper from total failure, especially Princess Florentina, who valiantly maintained a conversation, and Lady Evangeline, whose meaningless chatter was not only welcome but a relief.

Supper was a nightmare.

Mira had never intended to attend in the first place. She'd been throwing her clothes into her trunk when Princess Florentina had appeared in her room.

"Don't be foolish, child," she'd said when she'd seen the open trunk. "Not only is there no coach tonight, but travelling now in the deep snow is an impossibility. You will never make it to Cornwall."

"It is also an impossibility for me to stay here," Mira had informed her. "My presence here was a mistake to begin with. I apologise for being so unduly rude, Princess. But I must leave."

Princess Florentina walked to the window, drew back a curtain and pensively watched the snowflakes glide to the ground. "It was my idea, naturally, to invite you here." She turned to face Mira. "Atherton was almost out of his mind that night at the opera. Aldingbourne could barely contain him, and they almost came to blows. He would have burst into your opera box and caused a public scene there and then. I would not, could not, allow that. I had to find an alternative solution. So, I invited you, or rather Miss Cullpepper, knowing that she would take you along as her companion. After all, one could hardly invite a mere servant to a country house party."

Mira lifted her chin. "I have figured out that much, Princess."

"Yes, you are a clever one. I felt I knew you quite well

long before I ever met you. Atherton has told me much about you over the years."

He had?

"You have no idea how many headaches you have caused us, my girl. No idea at all. Not to mention organising this event at the last minute. The duke, his sister, the count, we have all made considerable sacrifices and worked very hard to make this happen. Do not let us down now."

They had?

"But why?"

She waved the question away. "I really must insist you come at least to supper. It is imperative. If you cannot bring yourself to do it for Atherton's sake, then at least do it for the sake of this old lady here," she stomped her cane twice on the floor, "who has gone to great lengths to accommodate you and who would be delighted to have your company tonight."

Mira was silent. The "old lady" who stood ramrod straight in front of her, with sharp, steel-grey eyes and hair whiter than snow, was indeed her hostess, and Mira had been unforgivably rude to her. Not only had she caused a scene this afternoon that must have embarrassed everyone within earshot, which was probably the entire house and all the servants in it, but she had been unaccommodating on the other days as well, looking for any excuse to avoid their company. The princess had been nothing but polite and kind to her, a mere maid, and she'd never let on in any way that she was aware of their social differences. She would suffer through the infernal dinner just for Princess Florentina. She owed her that much.

My Lady, Will You Dance?

So Mira had changed into a simple white dress with a blue sash. She didn't know that she looked vulnerable and beautiful and lost and that all the gentlemen would have fallen at her feet if she had asked them to.

She had not expected him to come bearing down on her as soon as she'd entered the room, to bow curtly and to offer his arm in icy silence. She'd been aware of every pair of eyes upon her, and an awkward silence had filled the room. For a second she had considered picking up her skirts and running. Instead, she'd put her hand on his arm, and he'd led her to the table.

Miss Pearson, bless her soul, had done her best to teach her how to behave as a lady, so she was quite confident that she could comport herself properly in this elevated society. But Miss Pearson had never taught her how to eat at a fully set aristocratic banquet.

It was overwhelming, to say the least.

The entire room glittered with crystal and gold. All the guests glittered too, all dressed in their finery with jewels and tiaras. Even the footmen glistened in their wigs and livery.

Between massive golden chandeliers, the table was decorated with greenery, etageres overflowing with fruit and fondant.

It was intimidating, to say the least, and for a moment she'd forgotten that she was angry with Kit and clung to his arm.

Dinner was served à la russe, which meant that the footmen served them one course at a time.

There was a bewildering array of forks and knives. Even though she'd spent hours polishing cutlery in the Cullpepper household, that didn't mean she necessarily knew when to use what.

The soup was simple. One ate soup with a spoon. Fair enough.

But when the footman placed a silver plate with escargots in front of her, she was entirely out of her depth.

The silver tongs lying next to her plate looked ominous. She'd spent time cleaning them when she was a maid. But how on earth did one use them to eat?

Her eyes drifted to Kit.

He sat there, handsome as sin, tall and broad-shouldered at the head of the table, a perfect gentleman of fashion from head to toe. The black cloth of his evening suit stretched across his shoulders, and his snow-white cravat was intricately tied.

She'd never seen him like this, but it suited him, the fashion.

He also looked like a stranger. His clean-cut jaw was slightly grim, his face immobile, as if carved from marble.

He was an aristocrat from head to toe, the Marquess of Atherton through and through. He'd wrapped himself in an aloof aura of haughty boredom and arrogance.

Mira scoffed.

That famous coldness of which everyone spoke. Did they not see it? It was just an act.

He'd always been an excellent actor, though he'd tended to excel in the silly, clownish roles.

The image of a lanky Kit in women's clothes during

My Lady, Will You Dance?

one of the guises arose from the depths of her memory. That day he'd dressed as a washerwoman, walked up to her, and bowed crookedly. "My lady, will you dance?" he'd crooned in a falsetto voice that had everyone in stitches.

He was playing a role, nothing more. A role he'd learned to perfect over the years.

It did not impress Mira in the least.

The real Kit was somewhere underneath, the Kit she'd known all her life.

And Mira was the only person in the room who understood he was merely playacting.

Not that it mattered.

Not that she cared.

She was still very, very angry.

She stared darkly at the escargot as the cogs in her brain went round, piecing all the puzzle pieces together one by one.

She'd known, of course, that his mother had been a gentleman's daughter. His father had been a clergyman who'd died when Kit was young, and that he'd had no one left in his family. Mira knew, because after Kit had disappeared, she'd tried to find his mother's relatives with little success.

Well, she'd been mistaken.

Evidently there must have been family somewhere. An old, crotchety marquess far away in the family line without a direct heir, for one.

And Kit, quite unexpectedly, had come into the inheritance of a marquessate.

A blacksmith who became a marquess. It really was

truly a most incredible story.

"Is the food not to your liking?" said a voice to her right. It was Aldingbourne attempting to make conversation. "These escargots in garlic sauce are really quite delicious, and I recommend that you at least try them."

"Very well." Mira picked up the tongs and stared at them. What was she to do with this contraption? If she ever wanted to get through this torturous supper, she had to figure out how to eat these things.

Her eyes involuntarily wandered to Kit again for help.

Immediately understanding her predicament, he unobtrusively lifted the tongs, clamped them together and showed her how to lift the snail. Then he lifted the two-pronged fork and dug into the snail, pulling out the flesh.

Mira imitated him.

Blast the man, but the two of them had always had an uncanny ability to communicate without words, as if they could read each other's minds.

Kit knew full well she was blistering cross and ready to cut him to shreds. So he respectfully let her stew in her own thoughts and made no attempt to speak to her. One word from him and she'd dump the foie gras on his head, regardless of whether the whole table was watching.

She had to grudgingly admit, however, that his table manners had improved nicely. The boy she'd known had mostly preferred to eat with his hands, both elbows propped on the table as he bit into a piece of Cornish pasty. He'd also liked to talk with his mouth full. Now, he handled the silverware dexterously, and raised a glass of white wine between two fingers before taking a lazy sip. Zounds, if he didn't behave like the lord of the manor.

But then he'd had seven years of practice at playing the lord, eating escargots and caviar, while she'd had to eat poor man's bread in the workhouse for the first few weeks after arriving in London.

Her eyes darkened again at the memory.

"Miss Taylor?" That was the duke again. "Your face looked unexpectedly grim, so I enquired whether the escargots have fallen in your disfavour."

"It is not the snails that are in my disfavour, Your Grace," she informed him, glaring at Atherton.

The duke coughed. "Ah, yes. Understandable, on some level." He bowed his head and lowered his voice. "Before making further judgements, however, would it not be conducive to reason to hear out the culprit?"

Mira looked at him in surprise. Had he just tried to put in a good word for Kit?

She narrowed her eyes.

Without waiting for her reply, the duke picked up his champagne goblet. "Atherton. What do you say, is an announcement in order?"

Atherton put down his cutlery with a clatter. "Indeed," he replied coolly. "Let's not waste any more time. There is no point." He raised his voice as he addressed everyone in the room. "As surely many of you have ascertained, there has been an unexpected development in my personal life lately."

He turned to Mira and firmly locked eyes with her.

"I am delighted to present my wife, the Marchioness of Atherton."

Chapter Fourteen

"I am not his wife!" Mira insisted for the hundredth time.

But no one listened to her.

They were in the library, and everyone stood about the room, talking simultaneously, ignoring her.

After the announcement, chaos had broken out at the supper table, with everyone attempting to congratulate them. Then the polite order of things had gone completely awry. The next course was skipped and pudding to be served in the salon. While the ladies retired there, Kit had taken Mira firmly by the elbow and whisked her out of the room to the library, where she'd attempted to box him in the chin in the manner he once taught her, but knowing her all too well, he'd anticipated her intention and ducked in time.

"Have you completely lost your mind?" Mira hissed at him.

"You can punch me later, my love. It was necessary. Sit here. Let's discuss this." He pressed her onto the sofa.

"I am not your love." She crossed her arms with a mulish expression on her face.

"You are and always will be, but we will discuss this later," he'd replied, leaving her fumbling for an answer.

Then Aldingbourne, Lindenstein, and Princess Florentina entered. After some argument with Aldingbourne, Evie and Rose joined them.

"I insist that I not be excluded now of all times," Evie declared. "After all, it was I who first saw Mirabel at the opera. I shall be there to watch the drama until the end. Sit here beside me, Rose." She patted the seat beside her. "Let the final act begin."

Princess Florentina said, "Mind you, it is not at all the thing to leave our guests unattended, but finding a solution to this matter is more urgent. Atherton, you sprang this on us rather hastily, I must say. I expected you to make the announcement at the ball, but what is done is done. We must revise the plan and discuss the next steps on how to launch the marchioness into society."

Marchioness? Mira had the vague notion that they were talking about her, but the cogs in her brains had stopped functioning after Kit had made that preposterous announcement.

Lindenstein sat next to Mira and took her hands in his. "Your hands are cold, *Liebes*," he remarked.

Atherton scowled at him. "Stop calling her that and stop touching my wife."

"I am not his wife," she declared for the one-hundred-and first time.

This time Aldingbourne had heard her. He whipped out a sheet of paper and spread it out on the table.

"This is a copy of the entry in the parish register of Fowey," he explained. He cleared his throat. "'Christopher Robert Taylor, blacksmith, of the parish, bachelor, and Mirabel Jane Allen, spinster, of the same parish, were married in this church by banns this fourteenth day of June, in the year one thousand eight hundred-and-seven, by George Knox, vicar. Signed with two witnesses, Mary Smith and John Williams'. It appears to be a valid registration in every respect, the groom being of age at one-and-twenty, the bride, still a minor at eighteen, having been given consent by her guardian, a certain Miss Leonora Pearson. Both parties were unmarried prior to the event. The residency requirement was met. The banns were read on three consecutive Sundays before the wedding. This is your signature, is it not?" Aldingbourne pointed to the paper.

Mira stared at the carefully crafted, childlike cursive that read Mirabel Jane Allen.

She furrowed her brow. "It doesn't say Christopher de Lacey, Marquess of Atherton anywhere. I married a blacksmith, not a marquess. It cannot possibly be valid."

The duke polished his lorgnette. "As Atherton's long-standing friend, I have, for his sake, spent a considerable time in studying the law to become something of an expert in all things marriage legal and otherwise. Here are the facts. A valid marriage had to meet the requirements of the Hardwicke Marriage Act of 1753, which in your case it did. A marriage was valid if the banns were read; neither party was married so bigamy was out of the question; consent or parental consent was given; the residency requirement was met; you were not closely related in the sense that you were siblings; you were both of sound mind at the time of the marriage."

Lindenstein lifted a finger. "Not to forget the most important aspect."

"'That being?" Aldingbourne raised an eyebrow.

Lindenstein grinned. "With apologies to the ladies, but I take it that the marriage was consummated?"

Lady Randolph clapped her hands over Rose's ears.

Princess Florentina snorted.

Evie gasped.

"Well, Atherton?" Lindenstein crossed his arms. "Was it consummated?"

"What do you think?" Atherton drawled. His green eyes twinkled devilishly as they met Mira's wide ones, daring her to deny that summer afternoon under the yew tree.

All eyes were on her.

Mira blushed to the tips of her toes.

She was in a quandary.

No matter what she said now, it would be wrong. Her first impulse was to deny it vehemently, but by tomorrow, she would be proven wrong. She could also admit it and hammer a nail into her own coffin.

She crossed her arms. "I refuse to comment," she declared, the bright red patches on her cheeks serving as a sufficient statement.

Atherton grinned, and she scowled.

"Knowing Atherton, let us assume that it was." Lindenstein leaned back, satisfied.

"Consummation is actually not a requirement for a valid marriage, and non-consummation alone is not a sufficient cause to annul a marriage in England," the duke explained, not at all put off by the subject. "Says the law."

Mira threw him a dark look. "You could have said that earlier."

He threw her an apologetic look. "Not that it matters because not even the old marquess, devil that he was, has been able to render this marriage void, even though he tried to pull all the strings and move heaven and hell to do so. Therefore, this marriage is valid and shall remain so until the death of either party. Case closed."

The duke had spoken. Having said his part, Aldingbourne proceeded to fold the papers.

Mira stared. "Wait. Did you just say that the old marquess attempted to render our marriage void?"

"Ah, at last." Lindenstein clapped slowly.

"Did you hear that? She just admitted it," Atherton said triumphantly.

Mira brushed them off with a wave of her hand. "Well?"

Aldingbourne nodded. "He tried to push through a divorce as a private act in Parliament, but failed, because Atherton was vehemently against it. Since adultery is the only ground for divorce, it stands to reason that it cannot be done if the husband himself adamantly claims that there was never any adultery. I also would have made sure the act never passed anyhow."

"Zounds," Mira breathed.

Atherton watched with interest as she put two and two together.

A young maid and a blacksmith got married in Cornwall.

The day after the wedding, the groom mysteriously disappeared, kidnapped right off the road.

The bride set out to find him... and found him seven years later, having come into a title, wealth, and land.

"So the old marquess had a fit when he discovered that his heir was already married. Not only that, he'd married, alas, a lower-class commoner," Mira mused aloud, completely forgetting her surroundings. "A misalliance. That must have been an embarrassment."

"Misalliance, nonsense. But it's an understatement that he was embarrassed." Atherton knelt beside her and took her hands. "The old devil nearly had an apoplexy. Lindenstein's right, by the way, your hands are icy." He proceeded to rub them. "The thing is, having failed to find a legal solution, he turned to other, uglier means." His face was suddenly grim. "He told me that you and Miss Pearson had died in a fire. I believed him. Only much later did I learn that he was responsible for all of it."

For a moment, the world stopped rotating. "Are you saying he was behind... he caused... he burned down our cottage and the school?"

He gripped her hands tighter and nodded. "I was too bull-headed and wouldn't cooperate, you see. He threatened to harm you, but even then I wouldn't listen. When he said you had died in a fire, I did not believe him. He said I was free to go and see for myself." He rubbed his forehead.

Aldingbourne nodded. "I am here to attest to the truth of his words. He was ordered to sever all ties with his old life. Including his wife. Atherton predictably refused. He made thirty-seven attempts in all to return to

My Lady, Will You Dance?

his wife, each of which was thwarted. Then the old marquess unexpectedly changed his tactics and allowed him to leave, and Atherton asked me to accompany him to Cornwall. We left the same day, and we found your cottage burnt. And three new gravestones in the cemetery."

Atherton gripped Mira's hands tightly, his face haunted by the memory.

"Three gravestones?" Mira frowned.

"Yours. And Miss Pearson's."

Mira shook her head in confusion. "And the third?"

"Our child," Kit whispered.

Chapter Fifteen

KIT HAD GONE WILD WITH GRIEF.

Aldingbourne had had a difficult time prying him away from the graves, where he'd collapsed, sobbing, and ordered him to leave him there to die.

Later, at the inn, Aldingbourne had arrived in the nick of time to wrestle the pistol from his hands. They'd struggled on the floor, and Aldingbourne had smashed a fist into his face.

"You must pull yourself together," he'd said, shaking him. "You must keep on living. She would have wanted that."

"What do you know?" Kit had howled, "and how dare you tell me what to do?"

Aldingbourne had dragged Kit to the wall where they lay breathing heavily. "I know and I dare. I know because I, too, lost my wife. I know the excruciating pain and agony that tears your heart apart. I know that a part of you died with her. And I know it will never, ever stop, the grieving. And I know that the only thing you can do is pick yourself up and carry on. Somehow you have to do the impossible, and through sheer force of will, you can. Because the alternative is to blow your brains out, which is the cowardly solution. You must find the strength to carry on. It is the only thing to do, and it is your bloody duty to do it."

"Go to blazes, Aldingbourne," Kit had replied. "I have lost my wife and my child, a child I had no idea I even had until we came here. I have no duty to anyone."

But in the end, he had done it. He had pulled himself together and done the impossible and dragged himself up and kept on going.

Somehow, he'd kept on going.

EVIE SOBBED INTO HER HANDKERCHIEF. "The story is not new to me, but I can't help crying every time I hear it. Poor Atherton."

All the ladies sniffled, including Princess Florentina, who discreetly dabbed at the corner of her eye.

Mira rubbed her forehead, dazed.

Kit was still kneeling before her. "It was only after the old marquess died last year that his secretary came forward and confessed that the old devil had hired some men to burn down the cottage. He was told they had only found two bodies, that of an elderly woman and a baby. They assumed that you must have survived somehow. Fearing the old man's wrath, for he was known to become violent when he did not get his way, they kept it a secret and told him the deed was done. The secretary only found out because one of the men who had been there confessed the whole story deep in his cups at the tavern. That was last year."

"So for six years you thought I'd died in the fire," Mira whispered with a sick feeling in her stomach. Where she'd always had the hope that he might still be alive, which had kept her going, he'd had no such hope. He'd really thought that she was dead.

"That's what I believed. It wasn't until last year that I actively began looking for you."

"We all helped, did we not?" Evie chimed in. "We turned over every stone in England, but you were just not to be found! And then one night, just like that, you were sitting in the opera box opposite ours. I was the one who spotted you first. I said, 'Look, doesn't she look like she could be Atherton's lost love?' I had seen your portraits, you know. Atherton had done dozens of them. You should have seen the look on his face. He staggered out of his chair and almost fainted. And now you are reunited for a happy ending to which I also contributed. Isn't it a splendid story?" She clapped her hands.

Everyone again proceeded to talk at the same time.

"But... I don't understand." Mira lifted a hand. "Who were the bodies in the grave? Who died?"

Atherton took her hand and looked at her with sorrow. "Miss Pearson and the baby."

"It's so very sad, isn't it?" Evie was about to cry again.

Mira shook her head. "But I don't understand. They did not die."

The whole room fell silent.

"What exactly are you saying?" Atherton asked slowly.

"I'm saying that Miss Pearson and the baby did not die. No one died. In fact," she took a deep breath, "it may please you to know that Miss Pearson and Clare are very much alive and well. God willing, they will arrive tomorrow." She looked him firmly in the eyes. "I've been meaning to tell you. You have a daughter, Kit."

Atherton, who had been crouching in front of her, toppled backwards and sat on the floor. "Can-can you repeat that?"

"Miss Pearson and Clare are arriving tomorrow. I wrote to them immediately after our first meeting here at the forge. And I've been trying to tell you about Clare. But somehow it was never the right time..."

Evie shrieked.

Rose jumped up and down.

Lady Randolph clapped her hands over her head.

"Congratulations, it appears you're a father," Lindenstein commented.

The duke did not say anything at all but crossed his arms, and a smile lit up his normally austere features.

Even the princess, for the first time, lost her composure and looked shaken.

Atherton's face was completely drained of blood. "C-Clare?"

"I thought it was an appropriate name." It had been his mother's.

He was entirely speechless.

"Would you care to tell us what exactly happened that day, my lady?" the duke interjected.

Mira looked from one to the other. "Clare was born the night the cottage burned down. But we were not in the cottage, we were at Farmer Smith's. His wife, Mary Smith, was our second witness at the wedding. You may remember that Mary was a most excellent midwife who attended almost every birth in the village."

Atherton merely stared back at her.

"Well, my husband had disappeared. There was a baby on the way. As it happened, Miss Pearson became increasingly anxious as my time approached and insisted that we move in with the Smiths. Just in time, too, because Clare decided to put in her appearance that night. And then they said there was a fire in the distance. They said the cottage had been struck by lightning and burned to the ground." Mira frowned. "Though not a drop of rain fell that night. The cottage was gone. Soon after Clare was born, we moved to Surrey to live with Miss Pearson's cousin, who was married to a clergyman, Reverend Barker. They were kind enough to take us in. Then Reverend Barker died, and money became tight. Clare and Miss Pearson stayed with Mrs Barker, but I went to London to keep looking for you."

London had been terrible. She hadn't found work at first. Nobody wanted to take on a country girl with no references and a baby on the side. With no money at all, she'd had the option of walking the streets or going into the workhouse. She had chosen the workhouse, where a week later Lady Cullpepper had appeared along with several other upper-class women and decided to do her Christian duty and hire a maid at a low wage.

"At some point after you'd left for Surrey, the old marquess must have had the fake graves made. I think we all agree he was a very bad man," Evie proclaimed. "But finding you all alive and well and reunited is a splendid ending to such an awfully sad story."

The duke rubbed his forehead. "The ultimate lesson being never believe any source of information without verifying it, even if it comes from one's secretary. It appears we are all at fault here for having believed the secretary to have been a reliable source of information regarding the body count, when the graves were all fake to begin with. He must not have verified what he was told and taken the words of a drunkard for granted. It is unforgivable, really. We might have been able to find you faster if we'd had all the facts straight."

"What happened, happened," Princess Florentina put in. "Let us not rehash the gruesome details. Ultimately, this story has a happy end, and as Lady Evangeline says, it is a splendid one indeed." She got up. "Having come to the conclusion that the marchioness is very much alive, and that the marriage is valid, and that there is a child to boot, may I remind everyone that tonight is Christmas Eve, and we have other guests in the house? Pull yourself together, Atherton. Fathers are made every day; it really is not such big a matter. Regardless of the familial matters here, guests need to be seen to. I insist they should not be neglected."

Chapter Sixteen

Everyone was dancing and singing and making merry. The Christmas fire crackled and roared within the hearth, its glowing embers casting a warm and inviting light upon the guests, for the footmen had painstakingly brought in the Yule log the night before, making sure it remained ablaze for the duration of the festivities. Under the fragrant boughs of the mistletoe, kisses were exchanged. The pinnacle of merriment was achieved when Lindenstein had pressed a kiss on Rose's lips, laughing, for both had been caught standing unwittingly underneath the mistletoe. Rose's face had been scarlet, yet she'd laughed along. As the evening advanced, the guests gathered for a spirited round of parlour games, the merriment echoing through the manor.

Mira, however, had slipped away during a particularly boisterous game.

She'd wanted to talk to Kit, but he was surrounded by men talking to him. He had appeared dazed for the first few hours, refusing to let go of her hand, but then Evie had taken her by the arm and insisted that she join them in the snapdragon game. Raisins were set alight in a shallow bowl of heated brandy, and the idea was to catch them out of the blue flames and into the mouth without burning oneself. This was done amidst much hilarity and giggles.

Mira's head was aching, and she sought silence.

As she stepped out into the hall, a group of young people descended the staircase, announcing their intention to play a round of blindman's buff.

As she had done earlier, Mira slipped into the corridor behind the servant's door, but this time she went down the stairs.

She found herself in the servants' hall and the adjoining kitchen.

It was well past midnight, and the scullery maid was still doing the dishes. The silver plates, cutlery and crystal goblets would be polished to perfection in the light of day tomorrow.

Monsieur Petit, a highly proficient French cook who ruled strictly over his domain, was sitting in a chair, fanning himself.

When he saw Mira, he jumped to his feet. "Milady! Is there anything you need?"

"No, no. I was merely..." *looking for the kitchen,* she'd been about to say. The kitchen had always been the heart of the house for her, a source of comfort. The essence of home.

She could not explain this to the cook, of course, as she remained standing awkwardly about the room, taking in the tables overloaded with half-empty dishes and copper pans. "Do you need any help?" she finally offered.

The cook's face was a study in horror. "Help? Milady wants to help? You can help by leaving the kitchen *vite vite.*"

"It's just that... would you let me stay here for a while, please?"

He frowned. "Can't sleep, perhaps? Would you like a glass of warm milk?"

"No, thank you. Dinner was quite excellent. I particularly enjoyed the snails."

"They are a specialty of my country, milady," the cook boasted.

"They were delicious. I was wondering..." She hesitated. "If you might have any fairings mayhap?"

The cook flared his nostrils. "Milady. I can offer you marzipan confections, sugar plums, charlotte russe, meringues, baba au rhum, apricot ices, syllabub, trifles, mince pies, and Christmas pudding, no, I take that back, I cannot possibly offer Christmas pudding because it will be served tomorrow after Christmas dinner. But isn't that enough? Do you have to have those, what do you call them, fairings? I have never heard of these fairings you speak of."

Mira described them to him. "They are simple ginger biscuits. Sometimes they are sold at the maid fairs in Cornwall, hence the name fairings."

"Ah. You mean simple biscuits of the kind eaten by the lower classes. I used to eat them as a child. I have not made them for decades. I consider them too lowly to be served on a marquess's table."

"You'd be surprised," Mira muttered. She thought for a moment. "Do you have eggs? Flour? Sugar?"

The cook confirmed.

"Ginger?"

He frowned. "We do not. I have used up the ginger for the various cakes and puddings for tomorrow."

"Well, instead of ginger fairings, it would have to be plain sugar biscuits, cut into shapes," Mira muttered. "I would be happy to make them myself."

"Out of the question, milady. I am overworked and have a Christmas dinner to prepare for nearly a hundred guests tomorrow, and I cannot have my kitchen disturbed by guests who have taken it into their heads to make commoners' biscuits in the middle of the night. I beg you, milady, be content with a few mince pies. I am a very busy man."

"I understand, indeed I do," Mira replied. "You have worked wonders this evening, monsieur. The dinner was delicious, and I have no doubt that you will surpass yourself tomorrow."

Mollified, the cook conceded, "It will be a masterpiece, my Christmas supper. We shall have canards a la rouennaise, turbot in lobster sauce, and a variety of roasted meats such as goose, beef, and venison."

Mira thought the selection was excessive. To her, a simple Christmas goose would have sufficed. "Dear me. As I said, you will certainly be working miracles."

"Ah. They say I used to be the best cook in all of France," he gloated.

"I'm sure you must have been! But assuming I stay out

of your way... if you could show me where the baking room is, I wouldn't bother you in the least."

He narrowed his eyes and considered her silently for one long moment. "Very well, milady. I shall make an exception this time only because it is Christmas. You may use my baking room."

Chapter Seventeen

THE BAKING ROOM WAS AN ADJOINING LITTLE ROOM to the kitchen consisting of a massive oven. Baking tins and copper pans were stored in the shelves along the wall, and a narrow table, smaller than the one in the main kitchen, stood in the middle of the room. This was where they made bread, pies, and tarts.

Mira tied a long linen apron around her dress and began mixing the ingredients for the dough.

She'd always loved baking. Working with her hands soothed her agitated mind and helped her think. She used to bake with Miss Pearson, back when they lived in their cottage. But as a housemaid she'd had no opportunity to do so.

After she'd worked out a smooth lump of dough, she realised she didn't have any biscuit cutters.

When she asked the scullery maid, the girl returned with a whole drawer full of moulds, biscuit cutters, and cake stamps.

Mira emptied the drawer onto the table and began to sort through them.

"Somehow I knew I'd find you here," a voice said from the door. Mira looked up sharply.

Kit was leaning against the doorframe, watching her.

"Milady insisted, milord," Monsieur Petit said, poking his head through the door. "I said no, out of the question, but milady wrapped me around her little finger, eh. Now she's baking when she should be celebrating with the other guests upstairs! What has the world come to?"

"It's all right, Petit. You may leave." Kit shoved the man out of the room and closed the door.

"Your cook says he's never heard of fairings, and he looks down upon simple sugar biscuits, which I find excessively odd." Mira lifted a square biscuit shape. "Really, my lord, you have every kind of luxury in this house but no proper biscuit cutter? Some of these look ancient and quite misshapen." She shook her head. "I need a snowflake. You can't have Christmas without them."

Kit looked at the pile of biscuit cutters on the table and inspected them. "You're right, there's no snowflake," he said. "I'll make you one."

He left, returning shortly with a hammer and a pair of pliers. He chose a larger, misshapen square and skilfully shaped it into a snowflake.

"Make it pretty. With six prongs," Mira ordered, "just like we had back home."

"I remember. Like this?" He lifted a small snowflake with six dainty points.

"Yes. Very pretty. Make a bigger one. Not too big. A medium-sized one."

"As my lady wishes," he murmured, and went on to make another.

Kit made snowflake after snowflake, and Mira rolled the dough and began to cut out the biscuits.

After a while, he set aside the pliers. "Let me do it. I've always been better at cutting out biscuits than you. You always leave too much dough between the shapes." That was true. He took the cutter and pressed it into the dough.

"I haven't done that since I left Cornwall." He looked at his work with satisfaction.

They worked in silence for a while.

"What's she like?" he asked suddenly.

Mira knew immediately whom he meant. She thought for a moment as she wiped her floured hands on her apron. "Cheerful. Lively. Never stops talking. Stubborn like her father when she puts her mind to something she wants. Cries if you step on an ant or if she sees a dead fly. Hates eating turnips, just like you." She smiled. "She has your eyes."

"By Jove." He drew his hand over his face. "How on earth did you cope all on your own? With a child, too?"

"I wasn't alone. I had Miss Pearson, remember?" Mira paused with transferring the biscuits onto the tray. "She took care of us every step of the way. Even though Clare grew up without a father, she had, at one point, three mothers, all of whom loved her madly. Me, Miss Pearson, and Mrs Barker. What more can a child want?" She smiled at him through a veil of tears.

"It must have been unbelievably difficult for you. I cannot even fathom what you must have gone through all those years." He looked haunted. "Do you think... will she... accept me?"

Mira took his hand in hers. "Of course she will. But remember, all she knows is that her father is a blacksmith. I dare say she will be as shocked as I was when she finds out who you really are. As will Miss Pearson."

"Tell me about her," he commanded. "Everything. From the night she was born."

Kit listened with rapt attention as she told him how she'd been born with a shock of black hair; how she'd been a quiet, good little baby, and how she'd turned into a little hellion by the time she was two. How both Miss Pearson and the Reverend and Mrs Barker had adored her, and how she had had a carefree childhood, even after the reverend had died and they didn't have much money, and she'd had to find a position as a housemaid in a London household.

"It made me sad that I could only see her once a week." Mira plucked at a biscuit and accidentally broke off a prong. "Because I was working with the Cullpeppers, you see. But one of us had to make a living."

"You said you ended up in the workhouse."

At one point, as she talked, they ended up sitting next to each other on the floor, leaning against the warm oven, draped by a woollen blanket, eating the biscuits they'd made.

When she had finished, she said, "And now it is your turn. Speak."

He rested his chin on his knees. "I resisted at first

when they took me in the carriage. But when the lawyer told me I was the prospective heir to all this, I confess I felt excited. I enjoy the advantages of rank and title, Mira. I won't lie. Who doesn't like being rich? But you see, I did not understand then that on the very day I was told I was to inherit all this, I'd lose everything about my old life. They changed my name. I wasn't asked. I wasn't given a choice. My opinion did not matter. I was stupid and naive and excited, and I thought they would let me bring you here. I thought they would send for you and Miss Pearson. But the old devil had a fit when he found out we were married. He tried to persuade me to divorce you. He wouldn't let me return to you. I tried to go home so many times, but they caught me every time. I was told to forget my old life. I was told to forget you. How could I do that?"

"It must have been terrifying," Mira whispered.

"It was..." He shook his head as he searched for the right expression. "I don't even have the words for it. Terrifying, but thrilling. Confusing, but also exciting. When you take your whole life and turn it upside down, and everything you thought you knew... all the people you love, suddenly they are all gone, and you are to be someone entirely different. That alone blows your mind to smithereens. Do you know what terrified me the most?"

"What?"

"All that power." He was staring at the baked biscuits without really seeing them. "I was just a simple blacksmith, Mira." He drew a hand over his face. "Thanks to some odd quirk of fate, I was suddenly responsible for all this land, all these people, farmers, tenants, servants. There's not only this estate, but three others."

"Hundreds of people to care for." Mira leaned her head against his arm.

"I had so much to learn. So many things I did not understand. Their way of thinking is so different, Mira. I've always been proud of what these hands could do." He raised his hands.

"They are talented hands," Mira said softly.

"I believed that too. But in this upside-down world of ours, in the *haut ton* in particular, a man who uses his hands to feed himself is not considered a gentleman. The first time I stole away to the smithy to fix a horseshoe, the old devil had me whipped."

"Kit!"

"A nobleman does not work. A nobleman does not use his hands." He shook his head. "As if it would not only taint the work he does, but his very existence. I am what I am because of my hands. I created with my hands. I made my livelihood with them. But I was no longer allowed to do that. Who am I if I can no longer use my hands? I am nobody, Mira. No one." His voice was laced with bitterness.

"You have lost your entire identity." Mira looked at him sadly.

"A gentleman can ride a horse. He can drive a phaeton, go hunting, shoot, gamble away his entire fortune, but he cannot work. Never work. They pride themselves in not moving a finger, yet they spend riches they never moved a finger to earn. It is a contradiction. An entirely unnatural kind of life."

"But rebelling only caused you trouble."

Kit nodded.

"Then you started pretending." Mira wrapped her arms around her knees. "And you became good at pretending. So very good."

Kit sighed. "What else could I do? If it had not been for Aldingbourne, I would have gone out of my mind. The things I had to learn! What to say and what not to say. All the rules, all the etiquette. All those books I had to read. I was just a country bumpkin who knew nothing. But Aldingbourne taught me. He taught me how to survive in society. I will always be grateful. I quite literally owe him my life."

Mira looked at him solemnly. "And Princess Florentina? What is her role in all this?"

"She is a friend of the family who took pity on the wild, grief-stricken animal that I was and talked some sense into the old devil. It was through her that Aldingbourne befriended me in the first place. We owe a great deal to them, Aldingbourne and the princess. And, most of all, to Miss Pearson."

"Yes, Miss Pearson," Mira agreed. The warmth of the stove enveloped her, and she began to feel sleepy. She rested her head on his shoulder. "Kit?"

"Hmm?"

She nestled against his shoulder and closed her eyes. "I am still angry, you know."

"I know."

"You left me and Clare, and we waited and waited and waited..."

"I'm so, so sorry," he whispered. "I will atone for the

rest of my life."

"But I am also very sorry. Because I broke all those vases. They must have been very expensive."

"They were ugly, and I didn't like them anyway."

"Still. I shouldn't have thrown them at you. It wasn't your fault, and you were suffering so much. And I am sorry I shouted at you and called you a chuckle-headed dolt."

"You are absolutely right. I am a chucklehead. Most of the time, especially in Parliament, I don't understand what they are saying. I just pretend I do."

"Kit?"

"Hmm?"

"I'm so sorry I didn't find you sooner."

"If only... if only I had not believed the lies they told me. About you being dead. All these lost years. I don't know how I will ever forgive myself for that." He hung his head.

"Don't." She took his hand, the one with the ring, and pressed a kiss on its back. "It wasn't your fault. None of it was. Do not feel guilty for what happened," she told him. "Do not look back. But let us look forward to what is to come. So much joy."

Kit wrapped his arm tightly around her and hugged her to him, pressing a kiss on the top of her head.

The next morning, Monsieur Petit found the Marquess and Marchioness of Atherton huddled on the floor by the stove, sound asleep, still hugging each other. A plate of half-eaten biscuits lay on the floor.

Chapter Eighteen

Horse-drawn sledges had pulled up to the main entrance of the manor and were waiting for the guests to climb aboard for the Christmas service. Hot bricks would be placed under their feet, with the ladies wrapped in furs, muffs, shawls and hooded cloaks, and the gentlemen in fur-trimmed greatcoats.

It would be a splendid affair indeed to see the cavalcade of grand ladies and gentlemen drive through the village to the church for Christmas mass.

Just before the guests boarded the sledges, a plain, unassuming horse-drawn carriage pulled into the driveway and stopped beside them.

A footman stepped forward to open the door and a wiry woman descended from the vehicle.

She stood ramrod straight, wrapped in several layers of shawls, a masculine beaver hat sitting smartly on her iron-grey hair.

Behind her appeared a bundle wrapped from head to

toe in shawls, and in the attempt to jump from the carriage, fell headlong into the snow.

The woman picked her up, brushed off the snow, and unpacked the bundle. Underneath five shawls and two coats, a dark curly mop of a head appeared. The child was wearing a simple, threadbare woollen coat that seemed too small, and mittens that were too big for her. She pulled them off and looked around curiously.

Seeing the ladies and gentlemen standing on top of the stairs, watching them, she turned away shyly and made a motion to hide behind the woman's skirts.

Until she saw Mira.

A squeal pierced the air, scaring up a murder of crows from the treetops. "Mama!"

Mira's heart stopped, then began to race. A little whirlwind whisked up the stairs, past the sledges, horses, coachmen, footmen, and astonished ladies, and hurled itself at Mira.

Mira dropped to her knees and buried her face in the child's hair. "Clare. My Clare."

"Look, Mama, look! I have lotht my teef." Clare bared her teeth and showed off a gap where her two front teeth used to be.

Mira tucked away the curls from her face. "So you have, my love. Since when?"

"Yethderday. First one fell out some weeks ago, and yethderday the other one fell out when I tried to bite into an apple. What do I do when they all fall out, and I shall have no teef at all? And it is Chrithmath!"

Mira tucked away the curls from her face. "They will grow in soon, my love." She looked up with a smile as the older woman approached. "Miss Pearson. I'm so glad you have arrived safely."

"I must say that was quite a trip, but thankfully uneventful given all the snow." Miss Pearson said as she handed the bundle of shawls to a footman.

"We saw deer!" Clare chimed in.

"We did indeed. But let's mind our manners, child." Miss Pearson looked at the assembled guests at the top of the stairs.

"Ooh, look at this pretty place, and all the pretty people."

Clare stepped in front of the three gentlemen standing at the top of the stairs: the duke, Lindenstein and Atherton, all three watching the scene with some bemusement.

"Which one of you ith my papa?" Clare demanded, leaving them all dumb struck.

THEY WOULD ARRIVE LATE for mass. But perhaps that was understandable, for it wasn't every day that the marquess was reunited with his long-lost love and little daughter, of whose existence he had not known until recently.

He'd stared, stunned, at the little girl who'd scrutinised each of the three gentlemen, only to look up at him with an adorable, wide, gap-toothed grin. "I think you are."

"I think so too," he'd replied.

"Kit Taylor, you wretch!" Miss Pearson lifted her stick as if to threaten him with a thrashing. "Disappearing like that, causing us a head and heartache to no end. I have aged twenty years before my time. Do you see my hair? It has turned completely grey, thanks to you. We shall have to have a word about that later. Let me look at you, my boy. I see you have put some flesh on those lanky limbs of yours." She patted his cheeks. "You may even have grown a little. Your mother would have been proud."

Atherton wrapped her in a hug and nearly lifted her off her feet. "Miss Pearson. You have no idea how delighted I am to see you. My world has not been the same without you in it."

"Nonsense, boy. Put me down and introduce me to your friends." She pointed her stick at the Duke of Aldingbourne, who stood next to him. "Who are you? You look important."

Atherton made the introductions. "Your Grace, may I present Miss Pearson. Miss Pearson, this is His Grace, the Duke of Aldingbourne."

She sniffed. "I've heard all about you. You dabble in foreign politics. I follow the news closely, you see. Do bring this miserable war to an end so that the rest of us can finally sleep in peace. But mind you, don't get yourself killed in the process."

The duke looked taken aback. "I'll do my best not to, ma'am."

"And you?" She met the unyielding gaze of Princess Florentina.

Once more, Atherton introduced them.

My Lady, Will You Dance?

The two women appraised each other, and it was clear that the princess had finally found her match.

"You have looked after our Kit all this time," Miss Pearson said. "I suppose I owe you thanks for keeping him alive and well, considering the circumstances."

"Considering the circumstances, indeed," the princess replied with a touch of irony. "It is, in turn, a pleasure to meet the woman who took in Atherton and cared for him when he lost his mother. I have heard a great deal about you. You seem to be a remarkable woman."

"Balderdash. One does one's Christian duty, no more and no less. But I see you are about to attend mass. Clare and I shall join you," Miss Pearson declared. "After all, it is Christmas."

FAMILY, the reverend preached, was what it was all about. The child in the humble manger, the embodiment of the birth of the Lord and the purest symbol of love. He reminded them that this sacred season was about coming together with those held dear, whether it be the bonds of immediate family, the cherished companionship of friends, or even the stranger sitting beside you in the polished wooden pew.

Clare sat between her parents, one hand in Mira's, the other in Atherton's. She'd fallen asleep as the reverend rambled on and on. Her head dropped on Kit's shoulder.

Mira saw the expression of wondrous tenderness on his face as he looked down at his daughter's dark locks, not daring to breathe lest he disturb her sleep, which made her catch her breath.

Their eyes met above their little daughter's head.

Mira's filled with tears of joy.

Family, indeed, was the true meaning of Christmas.

Chapter Nineteen

There was to be a glamorous Christmas ball to end the festivities.

After that, the house party would be over, and everyone would return to their homes, except for Mira, Clare, and Miss Pearson. Mira had not yet got used to the idea that she would be staying on at Highcourt Abbey, for it was to be her home now.

It was inconceivable.

"Sometimes I still think I'm dreaming," she had told Kit earlier. They were lying on the grand bed in the yellow bedroom, oblivious to the fact that it was in the middle of the day. "I'm afraid I'll wake up and find myself back in my little servant's room in the attic. I must get up before dawn and light the fires in all the rooms, clear the chamber pots and fill the pitchers with hot water—"

Kit took her hand wearing his ring and kissed it. "These hands will never have to work again—unless you want them to. It will be entirely your choice, because I understand what it feels like to be told that you are not allowed to work. But you have servants a-plenty now to do the work for you."

"You said you'd build me a small cottage, Kit Taylor. You ended up giving me a palace with servants. I never said I wanted a palace. You always go to extremes, don't you?"

"I still want to build that cottage." He raised his hands to study them. "Brick by brick. From the ground up. I've always wanted to do it, on my own. Just to prove to myself that I can. Maybe I will. On the other side of the park."

"Make it a simple thatched cottage with a little fireplace inside," Mira murmured into his shoulder. "You know, where we can snuggle up in front of it and roast chestnuts in the winter."

"Anything my lady wants. What else?"

"A small kitchen and two rooms."

"Only two?"

"One for us and one for Clare."

"I'll make four."

She playfully bit into his shoulder. "You'll end up building another palace! Besides, what do we need four rooms for?"

He lifted her hand and lowered finger by finger, as he counted. "A bedroom for you and me." He folded her thumb. "Then a bedroom for little Clare." He folded her second finger. "One for Miss Pearson."

"Ah, yes. She deserves a room too. And the fourth?"

"The fourth, just in case." He folded down the fourth finger.

"In case of what?"

"You know. Our next child."

She met his smouldering gaze.

"I missed seven years of my daughter's life. I have no intention of missing our next one. Not a second, not even half a second. Starting—right now."

"Oh," she said breathlessly, and he kissed her.

A wondrous while later he said, "I changed my mind. Four isn't nearly enough. I should add ten more rooms. Definitely."

CLARE HAD PESTERED and pestered them to let her attend the Christmas ball. Mira had wavered, as had Kit. But allowing children at a ball was simply not done.

"Out of the question," Miss Pearson had declared, and her word was final. "There is no place for children at balls."

"I'm afraid it will be very late, my dear," Mira had told her daughter. "You would be the only child there and after ten minutes you would be very bored."

"It wouldn't be boring if I had a pretty dreth and if I could dance," Clare had insisted.

Kit had taken her in his arms and whispered something in her ear, causing her to break into a huge smile.

"Promith?"

"Promise."

Clare skipped away, humming. She'd walked around all day, holding Kit's hand and introducing him as her papa to all and sundry, which included not only all the house guests, but also the butler, the footman, a housemaid, and the groom. She hadn't discriminated between people and chatted to all with equal volubility.

"It is nice that I have finally found my papa," she declared to anyone who would listen. "Because he was lost for a very long time."

Much to Kit's relief, she did not seem to mind that he was no longer a blacksmith but a marquess.

"She is entirely unspoiled. Such an adorable little poppet," Evie said. "I hope to have a little girl like her one day. But first," she pulled her face into a grimace, "I must obey my brother's decree and marry the old man."

After Clare had retired to the nursery without a single complaint, Mira asked, "What was it you said to her?"

"I told her that if she comes out into the gallery when they play the waltz, wearing her pretty dress, I shall dance with her. But only that one waltz, and afterwards she is to return to Miss Pearson in the nursery."

Mira smiled. "She already has you firmly wrapped around her little finger, I see."

"Not just her, but her mother too." He leaned down to whisper, "There will be a second waltz right after that, one I will dance only with you, my lady."

Mira wore a beautiful blue gown, which her abigail seemed to have conjured up out of thin air. Over a satin blue slip was a sarsenet overdress, tied with a wine-red ribbon.

She had never worn anything so beautiful before.

My Lady, Will You Dance?

Kit looked breathtaking in his evening wear, which seemed to be moulded to his frame.

Yet as she stood next to him at the ballroom entrance, she gripped his arm tighter than she normally would.

Kit understood immediately. "All you have to do is take a deep breath," he murmured into her ear, "and just let them talk. Nod whenever they say something, even if you don't understand what they're talking about. Smile and nod or even better, look slightly bored and do not reply to anything at all. That usually works and they will leave you alone. But as this is a ball, there will be little talking and more dancing, one would assume. I usually just do what Aldingbourne does. That seems to work best."

"If I were to imitate Evie, I am not so sure it would be for the best," Mira said.

Evie had dispensed with all sense of etiquette and was about to dance with two gentlemen simultaneously, one on each arm, when her brother came bearing down on her to take her away to dance with her himself.

Mira, who'd observed the interlude, commented, "I thought that was what this little dancing card was for, to keep track of who one danced with, to avoid situations like that." She took a little booklet out of her reticule. "It will take some getting used to, because at the assembly in Fowey we could just dance with whoever we wanted, remember? I also heard young ladies have to obtain permission to waltz. Why must things be so strict when it comes to dancing, especially when it is meant to be entertaining?"

"I haven't the faintest idea, my love. Perhaps you

should ask Aldingbourne; he usually has the answer to such questions. But show me your dancing card."

She handed it to him, and he studied it with a frown. "Please give me that pencil."

She handed him the pencil and he scratched out the names in the booklet and replaced them with his own. "There. All the dances are with me, except the one with Clare, and a country dance which you may dance with Aldingbourne. I am a jealous husband and will not allow you to dance with anyone else. I couldn't bear it."

"Really, Kit." Mira laughed, shaking her head.

"WHAT GRATIFICATION TO see them so happy," Princess Florentina said to Miss Pearson. The two ladies sat side by side on a sofa, watching and commenting on the goings on at the ball. "Atherton is smiling. I have never seen the man smile before."

"You have not?" Miss Pearson lifted her lorgnette, a gift from the princess. "The rascal lived for it. He did nothing but play childish tricks on all and sundry until his mother died, that is. When I took him in, he was so heartbroken I thought he'd never smile again. It was really Mirabel who saved him. The two of them became inseparable like milk and honey, and the whole village knew they'd be a couple one day. And then there was Master Williams, the village blacksmith, who taught him hard and well. Where would that boy be without Mirabel and Williams?" Miss Pearson shook her hand. "And myself, of course." She added with a sniff. Then she turned to the princess. "One might agree that this duke of yours has also played a considerable part, as have you yourself, of course."

"Oh no, my role in all of this has been more of a spectator," the princess claimed.

"Nonsense. Modesty does not suit you, Princess. Now teach me how to use this device properly." Miss Pearson lifted the lorgnette.

THE FIRST WALTZ came early in the evening. True to his word, Kit stepped out into the gallery where Miss Pearson was waiting with Clare. As the first strains of the waltz began, he bowed and Clare, giggling, held out her hand.

Then they danced.

Mira watched from the door with a lump in her throat, seeing the two people she loved most in the world finally reunited.

"If I may," a voice said behind her. It was the duke. "Your hand for this dance?"

"You reserved a country dance with me," Mira reminded him. It was the only dance that Kit had allowed her to dance with another man.

"So I have. And now we will waltz."

"You may regret that, as I have little to no experience of dancing it," she said.

"It will be fine." Aldingbourne said as he expertly navigated her across the dance floor.

"I wanted to thank you for everything you've done for Kit over the years," Mira said. "You seem to have been his rock."

"It is gratifying to see that he has found the happy ending he deserves. I know of no man who has gone through such devastating mental and emotional hardship as he has. It has not been easy for him to adapt to this new life. He deserves to be happy now."

"And you, Your Grace?" Mira dared to ask. "Will you also have a happy ending?"

Aldingbourne's smile was bleak. "Hardly. But then, I never experienced the epic love story that you and Atherton had. You were always meant to be together, weren't you?"

"We were childhood sweethearts," Mira confirmed. "Kit first proposed to me when he was thirteen and I was ten. Then he repeated his proposal every year on my birthday, until Miss Pearson finally gave in and said yes on my eighteenth. That was nine proposals in all. You know the rest of the story."

"It is rather surprising of Atherton, whom one would consider not to have a single romantic bone in his body. As for me, alas, there was never any romance in my life. My marriage was a typical one, arranged by two families. I saw my bride exactly once before our wedding day. On that occasion she was weeping." Aldingbourne frowned. "She did not love me. I certainly did not love her."

Mira stumbled, but he held her up with a firm grip of his hands. "Oh."

"My wife died eight years ago. And that was that." It sounded so matter of fact, as if he'd long accepted this, but there was a sadness in his eyes that seemed to belie his words.

"You are a good man. You will find your happiness yet, Your Grace," she said quietly. "I firmly believe that."

"You are an incurable romantic, my lady." The duke bowed as the waltz came to an end.

A second waltz immediately followed the first.

Kit stepped up to Mira and bowed. She looked up at him, happiness rushing through her.

He held out his hand, and there was a smile in his eyes as he said, "My lady, will you dance?"

Chapter Twenty

August 1814, Highcourt Abbey

"Now that this horrible war is over, it will be quite pleasant to be able to travel to the Continent again," Evie declared. It was late summer, and she and her brother, the Duke of Aldingbourne, were visiting Highcourt Abbey before they left for their trip to Vienna.

"As much as I am looking forward to it, I fear I shall be awfully homesick and miss you all terribly. I wish you could come with me," Evie fretted.

"So do I, Evie, especially as I have not seen much outside of England. I would like to travel someday," Mirabel said.

"Then why don't you come and visit us in Vienna? It would be so lovely! We could spend Christmas together. They say it is particularly beautiful then."

"I am sure it is, but I do not think it will be possible any time soon."

"Oh, Mira, come along, do!" Evie shook her arm. "I must finally meet Hartenberg, you know, the man I'm engaged to. He is at least twice my age, and he's an old military officer in the Austrian army. I shall die of boredom! I should like to have you with me to tell me that everything will turn out all right."

"But you have Aldingbourne with you, and Lindenstein too, right? How can anything be boring with him around?"

"Oh him." Evie huffed. "There's something strange about him too. Haven't you noticed? Nobody really knows anything about him, he just comes and goes. Suddenly he's in England, then back in Vienna, and he never tells one anything. Neither does Aldingbourne. Disobliging creature. I can't rely on him to take me out in society. Aldingbourne will be far too busy with this congress. It would be so much more enjoyable if you could be there with me."

"I'd like to go, Evie. I really would. But I really cannot."

Clare came skipping into the room. "How do you do? Did you know I shall have a brother or sister soon?" she trumpeted into the entire salon. Her teeth had grown back, much to her relief. "Isn't that fabulous?"

Evie stared. Then she squealed.

Mira blushed.

"Oh! So this is why you can't travel. This is wonderful. Simply, simply wonderful!" She hugged Mira. "My sincerest felicitations."

"Thank you. We are very happy. Especially Kit, of course."

"Although I am not at all happy with my parents," Clare explained. "I wanted an older brother or sister, and they keep telling me they will give me a tiny baby instead! I need someone to climb trees and swim in the lake with me."

"If you can be patient enough to wait, your little brother or sister will grow up and not be so little anymore, then they will be able to do that," Mira promised.

"How long would I have to wait?"

Mira thought. "Seven years, maybe?"

Clare groaned. "That's an eternity!"

"It is, isn't it? But it can be worth waiting for, my love. But look, your papa is waiting for you outside to play cricket."

Clare's little face brightened, and she ran outside to join her father.

Evie sighed. "Seven years of waiting is nothing. I have been engaged to Hartenberg and told to wait for him since I was fourteen. I shall be turning old and into a mummy myself before we ever get married. That is my fate."

"Speaking of marriage, have you heard from Rose?" Mira asked.

"Yes, she finally married her barrister! I am so happy for her. In the end, Lady Cullpepper came to her senses and put her daughter's happiness before her own desires. That is what a good mother ought to do. I want to be a mother like that one day, to put a child's happiness before my own. Just like you," Evie said.

Mira ran her hand over her slightly swollen belly. There was a dreaminess about her that had not been there before. She went to the window and watched Kit and Clare playing cricket on the lawn.

"Look how well they play. Shall we join them?"

Epilogue

Vienna, September 1814

Lady Evangeline, sister of the Duke of Aldingbourne, burst into the drawing room of their Viennese apartment.

"You will not believe this," she gasped. "You simply will not believe it."

His Grace, the Duke of Aldingbourne, part of the diplomatic corps accompanying Castlereagh to Vienna, where the Congress was in full swing, put down the document he was reading wearily.

"What, my dear, is it that I would not believe?"

"Catherine." She wheezed, holding her side. "I just saw Catherine outside. Walking blithely down the Kohlmarkt towards Michaelerplatz. I swear, Julius. I did! It was her!"

"Stop making such jokes. They are not funny," he said sternly. "I understand that Atherton's reunion with his lost love was the most romantic event of your life, and it has no doubt excited your imagination excessively. But such stories do not otherwise happen. Stop attempting to create a similar event for me. Catherine died eight years ago. I saw her body with my own eyes."

"But I swear on my life, Julius. As I live and breathe. I would never play such a cruel trick on you. It was Catherine. Your Catherine. The duchess. Your wife. Happy and healthy and very much alive."

"Impossible." He picked up his document again.

She tilted her head to one side, frowning. "It was the same figure, the same hair. Even the mole on her cheek. Do you remember? Only Catherine had that mole." She pointed to the right side of her cheek. "That slightly heart-shaped one."

His face had taken on a light shade of grey, and he lowered his hand with the document.

"I'd recognise it anywhere, even after all this time," Evie mused. "Except, you know what was excessively odd? When I went up and talked to her, she did not recognise me in the least."

* * *

When a penniless musician is told she may be an English duke's wife, a quest for lost love begins. Don't miss the Duke of Aldingbourne's story in *The Forgotten Duke!*

Also by Sofi Laporte

Merry Spinsters, Charming Rogues Series

Escape into the world of Sofi Laporte's cheeky Regency romcoms, where spinsters are merry, rakes are charming, and no one is who they seem:

Lady Ludmilla's Accidental Letter

A resolute spinster. An irresistible rake. One accidental letter... Can love triumph over this hopeless muddle in the middle of the London Season?

Miss Ava's Scandalous Secret

She is a shy spinster by day and a celebrated opera singer by night. He is an earl in dire need of a wife - and desperately in love with this Season's opera star.

Lady Avery and the False Butler

When a hopeless spinster enlists her butler's help to turn her life around, it leads to great trouble and a chance at love in this rollicking Regency romance.

(*more to come*)

* * *

The Wishing Well Series

If you enjoy sweet Regency novels with witty banter and a

sprinkle of mischief wrapped up in a heart-tugging happily ever after, this series is for you!

Lucy and the Duke of Secrets

A spirited young lady with a dream. A duke in disguise. A compromising situation

Arabella and the Reluctant Duke

A runaway Duke's daughter. A dashingly handsome blacksmith. A festering secret

Birdie and the Beastly Duke

A battle-scarred duke. A substitute bride. A dangerous secret that brings them together.

Penelope and the Wicked Duke

A princess in disguise. A charming lord. A quest for true love.

* * *

A Mistletoe Promise

When an errant earl and a feisty schoolteacher are snowed in together over Christmas, mistletoe promises happen.

* * *

Wishing Well Seminary Series

Discover a world of charm and wit in the Wishing Well Seminary Series, as the schoolmistresses of Bath's most exclusive school navigate the complexities of Regency-era romance:

Miss Hilversham and the Pesky Duke

Will our cool, collected Headmistress find love with a most vexatious duke?

Miss Robinson and the Unsuitable Baron

When Miss Ellen Robinson seeks out Baron Edmund Tewkbury in London to deliver his ward, he wheedles her into staying—as his wife.

(more to come)

* * *

NEVER MISS A RELEASE:

To receive a FREE GIFT, exclusive giveaways, review copies, and updates on Sofi's books sign up for her newsletter:

https://www.sofilaporte.com/newsletter-1

About the Author

Sofi was born in Vienna, grew up in Seoul, studied Comparative Literature in Maryland, U.S.A., and lived in Quito with her Ecuadorian husband. When not writing, she likes to scramble about the countryside exploring medieval castle ruins. She currently lives with her husband, 3 trilingual children, a sassy cat and a cheeky dog in Europe.

Get in touch and visit Sofi at her Website, on Facebook or Instagram!

- amazon.com/Sofi-Laporte/e/B07N1K8H6C
- facebook.com/sofilaporteauthor
- instagram.com/sofilaporteauthor
- bookbub.com/profile/sofi-laporte